T0147083

SAVED FOR BEN

BOOK 1

JACQUELYN B. SMITH

WESTBOW
PRESS®
A DIVISION OF THOMAS NELSON
& ZONDERVAN

WestBow Press books may be ordered through booksellers or by contacting:

WestBow Press
A Division of Thomas Nelson & Zondervan
1663 Liberty Drive
Bloomington, IN 47403
www.westbowpress.com
844-714-3454

Because of the dynamic nature of the Internet, any web addresses or links contained in this book may have changed since publication and may no longer be valid. The views expressed in this work are solely those of the author and do not necessarily reflect the views of the publisher, and the publisher hereby disclaims any responsibility for them.

Any people depicted in stock imagery provided by Getty Images are models, and such images are being used for illustrative purposes only. Certain stock imagery © Getty Images.

ISBN: 978-1-6642-6887-6 (sc)
ISBN: 978-1-6642-6888-3 (hc)
ISBN: 978-1-6642-6889-0 (e)

Library of Congress Control Number: 2022911124

Print information available on the last page.

WestBow Press rev. date: 07/27/2022

This *Saved for Ben* series is dedicated to my loving and nurturing grandmother, Ora Lee Woods; a second to none mother, Lillie Mae Wood; and my village. My grandmother and mother used every opportunity available to broaden my horizons and instill life changing godly principles in me.

God has connected wonderful people to my journey of spiritual growth. My village consists of those who have prayed, encouraged, and helped me during my journey of academic years, military service, and personal growth whether in Georgia, Virginia, Texas, or Florida. I am forever grateful for their love, support, and endearing friendship. Last but now least, to my son, Jeremy, a precious gift of God, who has inspired me to continue making a difference through writing for those who are willing to trust God.

CONTENTS

1

BEN WANTS TO WORK

It was another beautiful day in Fairville, Georgia. The sky was blue, the sun was shining bright, and the temperature was eighty-two degrees with a zephyr.

As Mary raised the window in the living room of the small two-bedroom house, she said, "Ben! David! I'm tired of cleaning up behind you. Mom is going to be very mad if this house is not clean when she comes home from work. Can you at least clear your books from the table? I've already made up the beds and swept the floor."

Ben said apologetically, "Sorry Mary, I got distracted."

Rustling through the newspaper, he continued, "I'm looking for a part-time job so I can help out. I'm fifteen now and I want to work. Mom works so hard, I want to help."

David interjected, "You know Mom is not going to let you work. She always says that you have to take care of me and Mary."

Laughing Ben said, "That was when you were younger. You're thirteen now and at ten, Mary takes care of us."

Mary smiled and said "I'm glad you realized that. Do you see anything in the paper?"

Ben shook his head and said, "No, not yet! I think I will walk around town after school tomorrow to see if there are any signs in the windows."

David said, "That's a great idea. My teacher said that advertising in the newspaper is expensive. Putting up a sign does not cost anything."

Mary shouted, "If they can't afford to advertise, then they can't afford to hire you either!"

David cleared his and Ben's books from the table. Then he set the table for dinner. It was almost six-thirty and Mom would be home shortly.

David asked his brother, Ben, "What are you fixing for dinner?"

Ben rushed into the kitchen to see what was in the refrigerator.

He exclaimed, "How about chili dogs with tater tots and some carrot sticks."

David said, "Didn't we have that last week?"

Mary ran in the kitchen and berated David, "How dare you be ungrateful. Mom works hard at that factory and buys food she can afford to feed us."

She looked at Ben encouragingly and said, "That sounds delicious Ben. Do we have any ranch dressing? Can you show me how to make it?"

Full of shame David apologized, "You're right Mary. I don't know what I was thinking. I'll go get the mail."

Ben showed Mary how to prepare the tater tots in the oven.

Ben asked, "How about we cook the hot dogs in the oven too. That will give us less pots to wash."

Mary exclaimed, "That's a great idea. I went over to my friend Becky's house. Her mother, Miss Tammy, cooked the hotdogs in the oven. They were delicious. She put aluminum foil in the pan first. Do we have any aluminum foil?"

Ben smiled and said, "That's a great idea, but I think we should put the oven on 350 degrees. That way, the hot dogs won't cook too fast. Mary, how did you get so smart?"

Mary laughed and said, "You guys got in so much trouble, I learned quickly what not to do!"

David ran in the house and announced, "I see Mom! She's walking in front of Miss Bessie's house. She should be home soon. I'm going to meet her and walk home with her."

He put the mail on the table and ran out the door. Ben looked at the mail. Some of the envelopes had 'past due' stamped on them. He placed the mail next to his mother's chair at the kitchen table. He put the chili in the pot to heat. Mary put the light bread on the table with the ketchup and ranch dressing, then ran out the door to meet Mom.

Ben practiced out loud what he was going to say to his mother, "Mom, I'm fifteen now. I think I should get a job. No! Mom, I'm fifteen now and I want to get a job. Is that OK with you? No! Mom, I was thinking that I could get a job after school, do you think that's a good idea? That's it. That's what I will say!"

Then he heard them all come through the screen door laughing. David was carrying Mom's work bag. Mary was holding Mom's hand. Ben ran to his mother to give her a hug and kiss.

He proudly stated, "Mom, dinner will be ready in about five minutes, I hope you are hungry. How was your day?"

Mom smiled and said, "Great, I'm hungry. I should be used to it by now. Every day when I walk that three miles from the rideshare, I work up an appetite! My day was great. It didn't rain, so I got to walk to the rideshare and back home dry as a bone."

Everyone laughed.

Mom smelled the air and asked, "What are we having for dinner?"

Mary answered, "Chili dogs and tater tots, Ben showed me how to cook them. We cooked the hot dogs in the oven!"

Mom laughed and said, "It smells delicious. Let me go wash my hands and I will be ready to eat."

Mary and David raced to the table to sit down. Ben put the food on the table, Mom walked back in the room humming. She always hummed when she was happy.

Everyone sat at the table, it was David's turn to say grace.

David prayed, "God, bless this food we are about to receive for the nourishment of our bodies. In Jesus name we pray, Amen!"

Everyone said, "Amen!"

Mom picked up the mail and glanced at it. Everyone passed the food around and started to eat.

Mom declared, "This hot dog is delicious. I like it cooked in the oven better. OK, tell me about your day. Mary, you can start!"

Mary laughed and said, "The hot dogs in the oven was my idea! My day was great. The teacher told me that I made the highest score in the class on the history test. She wants me to start thinking about an entry for the History Fair. I would rather enter the Science Fair, but my grades are better in history."

Mom questioned, "Are you having any problems with the white students since the school was integrated this year."

Mary answered, "No ma'am. I just do my work. Some of the white kids talk to me. I just mainly stay to myself until recess when I can see Becky and my other friends."

Mom declared, "I don't want you to be antisocial. I want you to be gregarious and friendly to everyone. It's their loss, if they don't want to be your friend. The Bible says, if you want to have friends, you must first show yourself friendly."

Looking at David, Mom asked, "How was your day? I heard that some of the black boys were having a hard time at your school. That there was fighting going on."

David said proudly, "Yes, you're right Mom, but not me. I too just keep to myself. In most of my classes, I'm the only black. I do my work, nobody talks to me. I do feel ostracized. The teacher has noticed that. She comes to my desk to make sure I'm OK."

Mom asked, "Are the white students being mean to you? If they are, that's a problem."

David replied, "No Mom, they're not mean; they are just not talking. I'm thirteen, six feet tall in the eighth grade. When we have physical education (PE) class, I can see them laughing because I can't play basketball. I'm not limber at all!"

Everyone laughed!

Mom said lovingly, "David, you get your height from your dad, but he couldn't play basketball either. You have other talents. You may grow up to be a tall lawyer or a tall business man. Just because you are tall does not mean you have to be an athlete."

Mom continued, "God will reveal what your talents are, until then relax and be proud of your height. OK?"

David smiled and said, "Yes ma'am."

Mom looked at Ben and asked, "Sweetheart, how was your day?"

Ben cleared his throat and said, "Mom, my day was fine. I'm doing well in my classes. I get along with my white classmates. I've been thinking. I'm fifteen now and I would like to get a part-time job. What do you think?"

Mom smiled and said, "You saw the bills, didn't you?"

Ben stood up and said, "Yes ma'am, I saw them. I was already thinking about working before I saw them. I was looking at the newspaper, but I didn't see anything. I plan to walk around town after school tomorrow to see if someone has a sign in the window."

Mom wiped her mouth with the back of her hand then said, "Ben, your dad would be very proud of you for wanting to work. I am too. I can't believe it's been five years since he died. I have some issues about you getting a job."

David said, "I told you Mom was not going to let you work."

Mom gave David a look. This was the look that we all knew meant to shut up and be still.

Mom raised her voice and said, "Don't put words in my mouth David."

Mom continued with a stern voice, "I think, it's a great idea, I just have some stipulations:

1. Your grades cannot drop. You are an A student, I don't expect anything less. You have to keep your grades up, so you can go to college.

2. You have to be home from work by seven o'clock pm. I don't want you working too late. That way you can eat dinner with us and have time to do your homework.

3. You can work on Saturday and on Sunday after church for a few hours. I don't want you working more than twenty-five hours a week.

4. I know you want to help out, but I will not take all of your money. The first ten percent will go to the church as your tithes each time you get paid. You can give me thirty-five percent of what you make to help pay the bills. You must save twenty-five percent, that leaves you thirty percent to do as you please.

5. Whatever job you choose, you must give one hundred percent to any task you are assigned.
6. You are not to take anything away from the job location unless it is given to you.
7. I want you to work hard and learn all that you can.
8. Show your boss that you can be trusted and depended upon."

Mom continued, "You have my blessing and support, if you can find a job that fits my stipulations and they hire you."

Looking at David, Mom smiled and said, "See, you don't know me like you thought you did?"

Everyone laughed. Mary touched Mom on the arm. Mom acknowledged her.

Mary said, "What does stipulation mean? I've never heard that word."

David explained, "Stipulations means conditions that have to be met."

Mom smiled and said, "That's right David. Ben, at any time that you can't meet my conditions, you will have to stop working. Is that clear?"

Ben acceded and said, "Yes ma'am. Thank you, Mom!"

David interjected, "Mom, when I get fifteen will I have those same stipulations?"

Looking at David and Mary, Mom said, "Yes, you both will."

Mom laughed.

Looking at Ben she said, "One more thing, finding a job will not be easy. It's 1972. You're a black teenager with no experience. Not many places will be willing to give you a chance. We live in Fairville a small town. Unfortunately, everyone is not very fair. There are not many opportunities for black adults, so don't be disappointed if you can't find a job right now. God will continue to take care of us. If it is meant for you to work, he will provide you with the right job. Now let's finish this delicious meal."

Everyone continued to eat their dinner.

Wiping her mouth with the back of her other hand, Mom continued, "David, if Ben gets a job, that means that you're going to have to cook dinner. You think you can handle that?"

David almost choked and said, "Me, cook? Uh, I guess I can. Will you practice with me or write down some instructions for me?"

Mom laughed and said, "Of course I will. We still have the recipe cards that I gave Ben when he started cooking."

Mary exclaimed, "I want to help too. I can cook a few things now!"

Mom smiled and said, "Yes you can help, but it will be David's responsibility to make sure everything is prepared."

Smiling David said, "Mom, I don't mind her helping. I may need it!"

Mom continued, "However, on the afternoons that Ben is home, it will still be his responsibility to cook. Everyone understand?"

Everyone smiled.

Mom said, "Ben, you will still have to do your other chores in the house. Just because you work does not eliminate your responsibilities around the house."

David interjected, "Yeah! Don't expect me to do them. I already have to cook."

Ben laughed and said, "I will Mom, I can't wait for David to cook his first dinner!"

2

BEN FINDS A JOB

After school Ben headed downtown. Fortunately, Fairville was not that big of a town. The high school was only one mile from downtown. It was another beautiful day, sun shining bright, with a slight breeze about eighty-two degrees. The walk was very relaxing. Ben practiced in his head what he would say to the store owners. As he walked through town, he did not see any signs in the window. So, he decided just to walk in and ask if they were hiring part-time help.

As he entered the Piggly Wiggly, he smiled. Talking to a cashier, he said, "My name is Ben, I was wondering if this store is hiring part-time help."

The cashier looked at Ben with a mean stare and nastily reviled, "No, we are not! And even if we were, we would not hire colored people in this store."

Ben was shocked at her answer. He replied, "Thanks for the information!"

He turned around and left the store. Next stop was the Rexall Drug store, he entered and smiled.

Asking the person at the cash register, he stated, "My name is Ben, I was wondering if this store is hiring part-time help."

The man at the register was dispassionate, somewhat flippant. He did not look up but answered, "Sorry we don't need any help right now, but possibly in the spring."

Ben said, "Thanks for the information!"

He turned around and sadly left the store. Next stop was the City Cafe. He knew blacks were not allowed to eat in the café, but was hoping they could at least work there. He opened the front door, cool air hit him in the face. However, as soon as he opened the door he was yelled at before he could enter.

The hostess yelled vociferously, "Can't you see the sign. What's wrong with you? You can't read! Only whites can come in here!"

Ben could not believe how hard finding a job was. He was so hurt that he started to just go home. However, he could not stop looking until he had checked every store in town. He had to be importunate. As he checked with each store, he got the same reply. Either they were not hiring or they were not interested in hiring a black teenager. He had not realized how prejudiced his town was.

He knew the city was divided into the have and have nots. Most of the 'have nots' were the black population. He knew the blacks understood the unwritten rules and just stayed in their lane. He did not think that looking for a job was against the rules.

It was now almost five o'clock. He needed to head home. There was a golf shop at the end of the street. Ben knew nothing about golf. There was a golf course in Fairville, but it was mostly used by the white population. Most of the blacks were not interested. Even if they were, there would be no way for them to learn the sport. As he got closer, he noticed there was a part-time help wanted sign in the window. Trying not to get excited, he started to walk faster.

He saw through the big windows an old white man slowly walking a customer to the door. The man waved goodbye and then headed back into the store.

Ben practiced out loud what he would say, "Hello, my name is Ben. I would like to apply for your part-time position. No, that does not sound good. Hi, my name is Ben Davis. Is your part-time position still open? No, that is not good either. I will say, good afternoon! My name is Ben Davis. I am interested in applying for your part-time position."

Before he knew it, he was at the front door. He opened the door which squeaked loudly and was hard to pull. The store was very bright, but it smelled like moth balls. The old man was standing at the counter. He was medium height, not fat, with a grey beard that was trimmed neatly. He gave Ben a mean look.

Ben gathered himself, raised his head, and said, "Good afternoon sir, my name is Ben Davis. I would like to apply for your part-time position."

The man stared at Ben, rubbing his beard looking him up and down. Ben was well groomed. It was hot and he had walked all over town, so he was a little musty. Ben smiled politely and waited for the man to answer.

The man said, "My name is Mr. Cason. I own this store, it's been in my family for two generations. I do need some help. How old are you?"

Ben smiled and said, "I am fifteen years old. I am in the tenth grade."

Mr. Cason said, "This sign has been in the window for six months. No one has applied for the job. Several customers have come in and out of the store. People pass the store every day, no one has inquired."

Ben stood still, trying to listen to every word Mr. Cason was saying.

Mr. Cason said, "Well, I am looking for someone to work no more than twenty-five hours a week: Monday, Wednesday, Friday, and on Saturday and Sunday. Do you have any experience? Have you ever worked before?"

Ben thought about it.

Then he said, "No, I have not worked in a store before, but I work at home every day. I have many chores and I have to cook dinner for the family Monday through Friday. My Mom does not get home from work until about seven o'clock in the evening."

Mr. Cason laughed and asked, "What type of chores do you do?"

Ben smiled and said, "I help my brother and sister clean the house. I take out the trash. I hang the clothes on the line to dry. I fold the clothes. My brother and I have to rake the yard regularly. I do a lot of different things in addition to doing the dishes and cooking."

Mr. Cason asked, "What type of student are you? What are your grades like?"

Ben proudly said, "I am an A student. I don't remember the last time I got a B. My mom is very serious about education. She planted the seed a long time ago that I would go to college. My goal is to get a scholarship."

Mr. Cason laughed and said, "I know most of the people in this town. Who are your parents?"

Ben stated, "My father was Bobby Davis. He died five years ago in a trucking accident trying to get home. My mom is Phyllis Davis. She works at the textile factory on the north side of town."

Mr. Cason said, "Yes, I remember your father, a tall man

that drove a blue 18-wheeler. I heard that your mother is a hard worker. I've never met her, but I have seen her from time to time in town."

He continued, "I would be willing to give you a try for one week. If at the end of the week, you have proven to me that I should let you work longer, we will test out a month. After a month, if I am pleased with your work, I will give you the job for three months. If I am still pleased, you have yourself a job."

Ben was trying hard not to show his excitement. He kept shifting his weight from leg to leg.

Mr. Cason stated, "The shop closes at six o'clock every day. What time do you get out of school?"

Ben cleared his throat, trying not to let his voice squeak, he said, "School is out at two-thirty in the afternoon. I would have to walk here, but I can be here by three o'clock."

Mr. Cason said, "That would be fine. I pay minimum wage which is $1.60 an hour. I will pay you every Friday for the previous week."

Ben said excitedly, "That sounds great."

Mr. Cason continued, "On Saturday the shop opens at ten o'clock, I would need you here by nine-thirty in the morning. On Sunday, I don't open until twelve noon. Is any of that a problem?"

Ben said reluctantly, "Sir, my family attends New Providence Baptist Church every Sunday. My Mom said that I could work after church, so I could not be here at twelve noon. I could be here at one-thirty in the afternoon. Is that OK?"

Mr. Cason walked around Ben, he saw that the young man was nervous.

Then he said, "That would be fine. I will see you tomorrow at three o'clock!"

Ben jumped for joy. He thanked Mr. Cason and extended

his hand. Mr. Cason shook his hand with a very firm grip. Ben left the store and ran all the way home.

As he ran down the street, only stopping to take a breath, he could not stop smiling. David and Mary saw him running home and ran to meet him.

David exclaimed, "How did it go?"

Mary asked, "Did you get a job?"

Ben stopped and screamed, "I got a job, I got a job!"

They all jumped in a circle in the middle of the road. Miss Bessie, one of the neighbors, was watching them through her window. They waved at her and ran the rest of the way home.

David asked, "Was it easy?"

Ben shook his head and said, "No! It was very hard. I went to all four grocery stores, both drug stores, the City Café, the movie theater, the laundry mat, and the dry cleaners. Either the stores were not hiring or they were not interested in me because I was black."

Mary interjected, "Mom said that would happen. Why did you go to City Café? You know blacks are not allowed to eat there?"

Ben laughed and said, "I knew we could not eat there, but I figured maybe we could work there!"

Everyone laughed.

Mary asked, "Then how did you find a job?"

Sitting down on the porch step with his siblings by his side, Ben said, "I was very tired and sad. Sad is not the word, I was hurt. Some of the people had been very mean to me. I was sweaty and had started to smell. I was about to give up and come home. At the end of the street I saw the golf shop."

David exclaimed, "I know that shop. I heard the owner was old and a racist. People said that he can be very mean."

Ben said, "Yes, he is old. I think he has to be at least sixty years old. I don't know if he is a racist. All I know is that he hired me. He needed some help. He said that the 'help wanted' sign had been in the window for six months and he had gotten no interest."

Mary exclaimed, "Ben! It's like the job was being saved for you. It was kismet. Does that make any sense?"

Ben laughed and said, "You're right, every stipulation that Mom had; Mr. Cason seemed to repeat the same thing. He only wants someone to work less than twenty-five hours a week. The shop closes at six o'clock every day, so I can be home by seven o'clock. He wanted me to start work at twelve noon on Sunday, but I explained that I had to go to church. I asked if I could come in at one-thirty. I was so afraid he was going to say no and take the job back."

David inquired, "What did he say?"

Ben said, "After walking around me and looking me up and down, he said one-thirty would be fine. Then he gave me this lecture about working for one week. If he liked my work, he would allow me to work for one month. After one month, if he still liked my work, he would let me work for three months. After three months, if he liked my work, I could have the job."

Mary jumped up and down with glee on the porch, "Ben, I'm so happy. I can't stop smiling."

David suggested, "Let's fix something special for dinner to celebrate."

Ben agreed, "Great idea. There are some drumsticks in the refrigerator. Let's cook them in the oven."

Mary asked, "Can we have some green beans?"

Ben laughed and said, "That sounds great."

David asked, "Can we bake some cookies for dessert? I saw some slice-and-bake in the freezer."

Ben agreed, "That's a great idea. I can also fix some potato salad. What do you think?"

Mary said sadly, "Ben, your potato salad is soupy. Can we have some yellow rice instead?"

Ben laughed out loud and said, "You're right, last time I put too much mayonnaise in it. We can have rice. Let's get started."

David said laughingly, "Well, I guess I better pay attention. I need to learn how to cook this meal, since I will be cooking on Monday, Wednesday, and Friday."

Ben hugged his brother and they all went to the kitchen. They all worked together to cook dinner and get the house ready for Mom to come home. When it was almost time, Mary and David ran down the road to meet her.

Ben yelled, "Don't tell Mom the news! I want her to be sitting down when I tell her."

Mary and David said, "OK, we won't!"

Ben leaped for joy in the small living room bumping into the couch and chair. He settled himself and prayed, thanking God for the job. When he looked up Mom, Mary, and David were coming through the door.

Ben hugged and kissed his mother then asked, "How was your day Mom?"

Mom replied, "It was good, someone took my work bag by mistake again. I hope they bring it back tomorrow. Last time that happened it was two days before they realized they picked up the wrong bag. I will have to take my lunch in a paper sack tomorrow."

Using her olfactory senses Mom smelled the air, then said, "Something smells good. Is that chicken?"

David exclaimed, "Yes ma'am and I made cookies."

Mom said, "Let me wash my hands and I will meet you all at the table."

After all of the food was put on the table and everyone was seated, Ben said grace.

He then said, "Mom! I got a job today."

Mom screamed with joy, "That's great. I have been praying all day that you would find a job."

David said, "It was not easy, some people were mean to him."

Ben said, "That's true. I almost gave up, but the golf shop at the end of the street had a sign in the window. Mr. Cason asked me a lot of questions about the jobs I had."

Mom asked, "Did you tell him that you work around the house and at the church?"

Ben replied, "I forgot about the church, but I told him about my chores at the house. He asked what type of jobs I do around the house. I told him. Then he asked me about my grades at school."

Mom could not stop smiling. She was glowing with pride.

Ben continued, "He asked me who my parents were. I told him. He said that he remembered dad. He had also seen you from time to time in town. Then he said that the sign had been in the window for six months. No one was interested. He asked what time I got out of school. I told him. He said that the shop closes at six o'clock every day."

Mary screamed with excitement, "Mom, then he could be home by seven o'clock, that was one of your stipulations."

Ben continued, "Mr. Cason was looking for help Monday, Wednesday, and Friday. Then on Saturday, I have to be there at nine-thirty in the morning. On Sunday he wanted me there at twelve noon. I told him that I had to go to church, but that I could be there at one-thirty."

Mom stood up and said, "Ben, I'm so proud of you. You handled yourself really well. How much does he pay?"

Ben exclaimed, "The job pays minimum wage, $1.60 an hour. I get paid on every Friday for the week before."

Mary screamed, "Isn't this good news Mom?"

Mom bowed her head and thanked God for the job and opportunity. She prayed for Mr. Cason that he would be blessed abundantly for giving Ben a chance.

Ben continued, "Mom, Mr. Cason said that after one week, if I had done well. I could work for a month. After a month, if I was still doing good, I could work for three months. After three months, if I had done good, I could have the job."

Mom exclaimed, "That is normal for people to be hired for a probationary period. This is above and beyond what I could have asked for. Let us all include Mr. Cason in our nightly prayers and that Ben will be the best employee he has ever had. Smelling this dinner has made me hungry, it looks delicious."

David said, "It's a celebration Mom! We cooked something special."

Mary said, "Ben wanted to make potato salad, but I told him that his potato salad was soupy."

David asked, "Mom, can you teach me how to make good potato salad?"

Mom said, "Yes, I can! Ben, when do you start work?"

Ben said, "Tomorrow at three o'clock."

Mary asked, "Mom, what does probationary mean?"

Ben said, "The first thing I will buy with my money is a dictionary for you Mary?"

Everyone laughed.

3

WORK DAYS NEED A PLAN

It was finally the last class of the day, Ben was so excited about going to work. He had to make himself concentrate on the teacher. He thought about what he would do with his pay. He could not believe that he would be getting paid every week. He would have money to buy gifts and even buy ice cream when the truck came through the neighborhood. That was a luxury, his family could not afford.

He was daydreaming so much that he was not sure what his history teacher, Mr. Harris, was talking about. He looked around the room and could not figure out what was going on. Everyone was writing something down. He raised his hand.

Mr. Harris said, "Yes Ben, you have a question?"

Ben said shamefully, "Mr. Harris, I am sorry. I was daydreaming. Can you repeat the assignment?"

Mr. Harris smiled and said, "Ben, it takes a lot of courage to admit that you were not paying attention. Don't let it happen again! Please complete the assignment on page twenty-five."

Ben smiled and said, "Thank you."

Ben rushed to complete the assignment just before the bell

rang. He turned in his assignment and walked fast to get out of the building. As he entered the parking lot, it started to rain. He did not have an umbrella or a rain poncho. He thanked God that it was not raining too hard. He ran when he could and walked fast trying to protect his textbooks. When he finally arrived at the golf shop, he was soaked. Mr. Cason was looking out the window and saw Ben running. He met Ben at the door with an old towel.

Ben thanked him for the towel then said, "I guess I have to start planning for the weather."

Mr. Cason laughed and said, "Yeah, but this rain came out of nowhere. The weather man did not say anything about it on the news this morning. The bathroom is right over there, go get yourself cleaned up."

Ben asked, "Is that the colored restroom? How much do I have to pay to use it?"

Mr. Cason looked Ben in the eyes and said, "I only have one restroom here and you are welcome to use it whenever you need to. There is no fee. Just clean up after yourself. Better yet, that will be one of your responsibilities, you have to keep this restroom clean. I expect you to check it when you come to work and check it when you leave to make sure the toilet and sink are cleaned and the floor is swept. You can mop the floor before you leave, so it can be fresh for the next day. All the materials you will need are in the storage room."

Ben smiled and said, "Yes, sir!"

Ben quickly cleaned himself up and cleaned the restroom.

After he was finished, he asked, "Mr. Cason what would you like for me to do next?"

Mr. Cason said firmly, "Let me review your work first!"

He went to the restroom to find it smelling clean of disinfectant. He lifted the toilet seat and checked the sides of the toilet to make sure it had been cleaned. He saw that the sink and mirror had been wiped down. However, there was still trash in the trash can.

Mr. Cason said, "You did a great job in cleaning the restroom. There is some trash in the trash can. I expect for the trash can to be emptied at the end of the day, unless it is full. If it is full, please empty it."

Ben replied, "Yes sir!"

Mr. Cason walked to the storage room, Ben followed.

Mr. Cason stated, "This storage room is a mess. At one time it was very organized. However, I am older now and I have not been able to keep up. However, because it is unorganized, I can't find anything anymore. I don't expect you to finish anytime soon. I do want you to work on this storage room every day. You're a smart boy, so organize it however you think is best. I would like labels everywhere, so I can find things. If you don't know what something is, just ask me. I believe in asking questions, so don't feel that you can't ask me anything. I am here to abet you. I will give you a marker, some tape, and paper for you to make the labels. I will also give you a copy of my inventory list, so you can use the correct nomenclature. I don't want any misnomers. How is your handwriting?"

Ben said proudly, "My penmanship is excellent sir!"

Mr. Cason laughed and said, "I figured it was! So, for the rest of the day you can work here in the storage room. You can take a break as you need to. That door over there, leads to the outside if you need some air. You can also prop it open if it gets too hot back here. The front part of the store has air condition, but not back here."

Ben worked hard for the next few hours trying to organize the storage area. There were shelves all along the walls with bins. He started to put the like objects together and move the bigger objects to areas of the room that made sense. As he worked, he got thirsty. It had stopped raining, so he stepped out of the back door and found a water faucet with a hose.

As he was drinking water from the hose, Mr. Cason yelled loudly, "What are you doing?"

Afraid he said, "I got thirsty. So, I was drinking some water."

Mr. Cason said, "Ben, you do not have to drink water from the water hose. I have water inside that you can drink. Did you not see the water fountain next to the restroom?"

Ben bent down to turn the water faucet off.

He looked at Mr. Cason and replied, "Yes sir, I saw it. I figured that was for white people, even though it did not have a sign. Other places in town have signs that say, 'white only or colored only'. So, since I did not see a sign, I assumed it was white only."

Mr. Cason walked toward Ben putting his hand on his shoulders and said, "Ben, I have seen those signs too. I don't believe things should be separate but equal. You're a human being just like me right. Is your blood red? Do you pee standing up like me?"

Ben laughed and said, "Yes sir!"

Mr. Cason continued, "Then I consider you the same as me. When you are in this store, you don't have to feel inferior. I will do whatever I can to help you and treat you with respect."

Ben smiled and said, "I appreciate that sir!"

As he was walking back into the building, Mr. Cason said, "The storage room is looking great. Get back to work!"

Ben continued working hard in the storage room.

Mr. Cason said, "It's six o'clock and the store is closed. There are a few things that I need to do to prepare the store for the next day. You can go now. I am very pleased with your work ethic. Tomorrow is Thursday, I will see you on Friday after school."

Ben was tired, but elated. He smiled, grabbed his textbooks, and said, "Good night Mr. Cason. I will see you Friday."

As Ben walked home, he reflected on his first day of work. He realized that he was walking slowly. He tried to walk faster, but he was very tired. As he turned to go down his street, Mary and David came running to meet him. David took his textbooks. Ben was happy to give them up, they were getting heavy.

Mary declared, "Ben, you look tired!"

Ben said, "I am tired!"

David exclaimed, "It's six-thirty, you beat Mom home!"

As Ben was walking up the steps, he said, "Let me go get cleaned up before Mom gets here, I stink!"

As he was coming out of the bathroom, Mom walked through the door with David and Mary by her side. He greeted his mother lovingly, smelling fresh and clean. After his Mom washed her hands, they all sat at the table for dinner. Mary said grace.

Mom started her regular inquisitions, "Mary, how was your day?"

Mary quickly said, "Mom it was great. I pass. I want hear about Ben's day."

Mom laughed, looked at David, and then said, "This meal looks delicious. What is this white stuff?"

David said, "That's mashed potatoes. They look funny, but I think they taste good. I added some cheese."

After tasting the mashed potatoes, Mom exclaimed, "You're right, they do taste good. Your pork chops are very moist and the carrots are sweet. Did you add sugar?"

David smiled and said, "Just a little bit. I also added butter and a little milk."

Ben said, "David, this meal is hearty and delicious. I was very hungry. I understand now how Mom works up an appetite when she walks home from the rideshare."

Mom said, "David, you did a great job on this meal. You have the makings of a chef."

With her mouth full Mary said, "I like these funny looking potatoes. They are good. Can I have some more?"

While putting more potatoes on Mary's plate Mom said, "They look funny because you did not add enough milk and stir them enough. Great job! Now, how was your school day?"

David said, "It was great. We have only been in school for two weeks and I can still change classes if I want. Can I change my schedule and sign up for Home Economics?"

Mom smiled and asked, "David, what class do you want to give up?"

David said, "PE!"

Mom smiled and said, "I don't mind you changing your class. Do many guys take Home Economics? When I went to school, that was a class for girls."

David said, "I asked my guidance counselor the same thing. She said currently there are three other boys in the class, so I would not be the only boy."

Ben said, "I know a few guys that are taking the Home Economics class in high school. They like it. One of the guys just wanted to meet girls though."

Everyone laughed.

David said, "My counselor also warned me that the Home Economics teacher can be very censorious."

Mom asked, "What does that mean?"

David said, "I had to look it up in the dictionary myself. It means severely critical."

Everyone laughed.

Mom said, "If that is what you are interested in, I think it will be fine. Do I need to sign anything?"

David replied, "No ma'am, I just have to tell my counselor tomorrow. Thanks Mom! I really liked cooking dinner. I was thinking about it all day. I planned the menu. I also went to the library and skimmed through a few cook books."

Mom said, "That's great, this may be one of your talents!"

Mom looked at Ben and said, "Tell us about your first day of work."

Ben smiled and said, "Overall, it was great. Even though it was only three hours, it was tiring. After school it started to rain, so by the time I got to the golf shop I was soaked. I got there before three o'clock. Mr. Cason met me at the door with a towel."

Surprised Mom said, "That was very nice of him."

Ben continued, "I know. Then he let me use the restroom to clean myself up."

David asked, "Was the colored restroom outside? Did he charge you to use it like the Dime Store does?"

Ben smiled and said, "No, he only has one restroom and he told me that I was free to use it whenever I needed to. One of my responsibilities is to keep the restroom clean and mop at the end of the day."

David said, "He doesn't sound like a racist or an aristocrat!"

Ben continued, "He is definitely not a racist! He is a very nice, old man. Then I had to clean and organize the storage room. He has given me free rein to organize how best I see fit. It's really messy. I don't have to finish immediately, but I have to work on it a little every day."

Mom said, "That's wonderful to hear. I don't know the man, but I will continue to pray that he treats you right."

Leaning forward Ben continued, "Let me tell you what happened next. I was organizing the storage room. I got thirsty so I went out the back door to find the water faucet. I was drinking from the water hose, Mr. Cason comes out the door yelling at me. What are you doing?"

Mary exclaimed, "Why? What did you do?"

Ben continued, "He really scared me. I told him I was thirsty and was drinking water. He said 'didn't you see the water fountain in the shop next to the restroom'. I told him that I did, but I thought it was for white people. Even though there was not a sign, I told him in other stores in town there are signs for white and colored."

Everyone stopped eating to listen to the story.

Ben continued, "Mr. Cason said that he had seen the signs too, however, he did not agree with separate but equal. He asked me if my blood was red. He asked if I peed standing up. If so, I was just like him. He said that in this store he would always treat me with respect and that I should never feel inferior."

Mom asked, "What did you say?"

Ben said, "I said that I appreciate that. Then he told me the storage room was looking good and to get back to work."

Mom said, "He sounds like a really nice man. I have run into some white people at the textile plant that are nice to me too. They also treat me with respect. Of the seven people that will stop at the ride share to give me a ride to the factory, about five of them are white people. We know that all white people are not bad, prejudiced, or hypocritical. There are many that work with the Civil Rights Movement. I'm so glad to hear that Mr. Cason is one of the nice ones. God answers prayer above and beyond what we could ask or think."

Ben continued, "At six o'clock he told me he was happy with my work and that I could go home. He would see me on Friday. I said goodbye and left."

Mom said, "That's a great first day. Continue to do your best, but don't take anything for granted. We do need to get you a rain poncho. I have one and it really keeps me dry."

4

HARD WORK PAYS OFF

Ben worked at the golf shop on Friday afternoon after school. David cooked another fabulous, healthy meal for dinner. On Saturday morning, Ben was up early finishing up some homework and doing his other chores before work.

With the radio playing in the background Mom yelled, "Ben, hurry up! Your breakfast is ready. You need to leave this house no later than nine o'clock."

Ben rushed in the kitchen, "Mom, the sausage smells good. I will just make me a couple of sandwiches for breakfast."

Mom smiled and said, "OK, here are some eggs. Take your time to eat, I don't want you to get indigestion. I made you and Mr. Cason peanut butter and jelly sandwiches for lunch. I put an apple and an orange in your bag too with a few of those cookies that David made."

Smiling Ben said, "Thanks Mom, I may have to get me a work bag like you."

Mom laughed and said, "David and I are going grocery shopping today. That boy is really serious about cooking. He showed me all of these recipes last night. I told him that we can't afford that type of food. So, we will be looking through the aisles to see if we can find some compromises or good deals."

Ben ate his breakfast sandwiches, then kissed his mother goodbye, and ran out the door. He was eager to get to work. He realized that he enjoyed working, but he really enjoyed spending time with Mr. Cason. He never had a person other than his family to be so patient with him or show genuine concern about him. Of course, the people at church showed him love, but this was different. As he walked through the golf shop door, Mr. Cason was waiting behind the counter.

Ben said, "Good morning Mr. Cason!"

Mr. Cason smiled and said, "Good morning Ben, this is your third day of work and you have been on time each day. That's a great habit, keep it up."

Ben went straight to the restroom to make sure it was clean and that he did not overlooked anything last night. Then he headed to the storage room to start work.

Mr. Cason entered the storage room and said, "Ben, before you get started, I want to show you how to do inventory."

Ben was eager to learn all that he could. They spent most of the morning going over the different products, vendors, ordering forms, and frequency of when items needed to be ordered. Together they set up a system that was easy for Ben to follow and documented all the information that he would need. Customers came in regularly. Whenever a customer came into the store, Ben would busy himself with things in the storage room

It was around one o'clock, Mr. Cason asked, "Ben, did you bring anything for lunch?"

Ben smiled and said, "Yes sir, my Mom fixed me a lunch. I also have some for you if you like."

Mr. Cason asked, "For me?"

Ben said, "Yes sir. My mother gave me a sandwich and a piece of fruit for you and the same for me."

Surprised, Mr. Cason said, "Well, I guess I can't turn down a lunch made just for me."

Ben smiled, "It's not a lot."

Ben took out the sandwich that had been wrapped lovingly in wax paper.

Ben inquired, "Would you like the apple or the orange?"

Mr. Cason laughed and said, "I better eat the orange, my teeth are not as young as yours!"

As Mr. Cason unwrapped his sandwich, he thought about how no one had shared their lunch with him in decades. His wife died over twenty years ago. He did not have any children. He mostly kept to himself. Most of the other store owners did not have the same social outlook as he did or they were hedonists. He had a couple of buddies he played golf with when he was younger, but they were all too old for that now and some of them had died. As Mr. Cason bit into the peanut butter and jelly sandwich, he closed his eyes. Thinking back to his childhood, he chewed slowly enjoying every bite.

Mr. Cason opened his eyes and said, "This sandwich is delicious. It has the correct ratio of peanut butter to jelly. The bread is fresh, I could eat two more of these."

Laughing Ben said, "I know. My mom makes a sandwich like she is making a fancy meal. She never rushes. My brother, David, made these cookies."

After they had both finished their delicious lunch, Mr. Cason stated, "OK, next Saturday, lunch is on me. How about a ham sandwich with some Golden Flake potato chips?"

Ben laughed and said, "That sounds great!"

Mr. Cason said, "Ben, there is one more assignment that I want to show you today."

Ben cleaned up the trash quickly, then announced, "Yes sir, I'm ready."

Mr. Cason showed Ben the display case that was near the cash register.

He explained, "This display case is used to hold the putter, driver, or special golf club of the month. I always try to spotlight different golf clubs every month. This marketing strategy has worked very well for me over the years. I sell more of the clubs that are on this display than any other club during that month. It's amazing how marketing works. I also provide great customer service without touting."

He continued, "This display case has been in my family for several years. When my father opened this golf shop back in the 1901, he put the display case here. This display case is very important to me Ben."

Ben smiled and said, "I'm sure it is. I have never seen anything this old. It's an antique."

Mr. Cason said, "Your job will be to burnish it. Do you know what that means?"

Ben said, "Yes sir, it means to polish by rubbing."

Mr. Cason smiled and said, "That's correct. I want you to take this cloth every week and burnish it. This cannot be a rush job. You can take it in the storage room if you like, get a chair, and take your time. If you do it correctly, it should take you at least forty minutes each time. I would like this display case polished every weekend. You can pick either day, but I want it ready for Monday."

Ben watched Mr. Cason rub the display case with the cloth, going in a circular pattern. He pointed out that it should be polished from the top to the bottom. The entire case is made of the same material.

Mr. Cason said, "It has not been polished for a long time now. I have not had the energy to keep it up. Now that you are here, I look forward to seeing it restored to its former glory. You cannot wet this cloth. There is no product to be used. You are only to use this cloth, you can fold it, turn it over, or ball it up. However, you are to only use this cloth. I know it looks dirty, but that's OK. Do you understand?"

Ben smiled and nodded his head.

Mr. Cason said, "The first time it may take you much longer, but take your time. I am not in a rush."

Ben took the cloth from Mr. Cason then asked, "Am I to rub like this or should I rub harder?"

Mr. Cason smiled and said, "Rub a little harder, as you rub you will see how much force you need to apply. Don't worry this is not breakable, but it is very precious."

Ben asked, "Is it heavy?"

Mr. Cason smiled and replied, "Well, it's not light, but a strong boy like you can pick it up."

Ben picked up the display case and took it to the storage room. He got a chair and started to burnish. Mr. Cason put a radio in the storage room and turned it on. Ben listened to the music while he worked.

On Sunday after church Ben rushed to work. He began his day with the restroom, then worked in the storage room a little while. After that he continued to work on the display case. He noticed how beautiful it was. He was very proud of his efforts. It was looking better. Mr. Cason commented on his progress. Ben worked hard to finish the display case. It had to be ready for Monday. Not many stores were open on Sunday, but it was a busy day for the golf shop. Ben was thankful for the radio, it made time go by much quicker. Whenever, he took a break, he would stretch his hands. They were getting tired and stiff. It was now five o'clock. Ben finished burnishing the display case.

He proudly declared, "Mr. Cason, Mr. Cason! I finished!"

When Mr. Cason walked into the storage room, he started crying. He remembered the first time he had to polish that display case. He wiped his tears with the white handkerchief that he kept in his pocket.

He said, "Ben, you have done a marvelous job. It looks brand new. When I was a child, one of my jobs was to burnish this display case. I don't think I ever did this well of a job."

Ben laughed and said, "I think it will take a week for me to get all of the feeling back in my fingers."

Mr. Cason said, "Yeah, but because you have done such a good job, it won't ever take you this long again. Let's move it to the front."

Mr. Cason picked up the case with pride, he was so happy. Ben was happy too. Mr. Cason had never talked about his family.

Ben asked, "Mr. Cason, when did your father pass away?"

Mr. Cason said, "He died when I was forty-one years old. I am now eighty so that was thirty-nine years ago. He had a bad heart. My mother died before that. She died when I was thirty-two. My wife and I took care of my dad until he died."

Ben stated, "I did not know that you were married?"

Mr. Cason said, "My wife died twenty years ago. I miss her dearly."

Ben was afraid to ask any more questions, but he had to know. He asked, "Mr. Cason, do you have any children?"

Mr. Cason looked at Ben and said, "No, we never had any children. That is my one regret. It is not that we didn't want any, but it was not meant to be."

Ben said, "Mr. Cason, I have been working here almost a week. You have been very nice to me. Can I continue to work for you for the next month?"

Mr. Cason laughed louder than Ben had ever heard him laugh.

He said, "Ben, you have done excellent work for me. I could not be more pleased. As of this moment, your probationary period is over. You have a job with me as long as you want."

Ben tried to hold his excitement, then he said, "Mr. Cason, thank you so much for this opportunity. I won't let you down."

Mr. Cason said, "It's almost six o'clock, start performing your closing checklist and then you can go."

Ben cleaned up the areas he had out of order. He mopped the bathroom floor, then looked at the calendar to make sure he had completed the order forms for the orders that needed to be placed on Monday.

When he finished, he said, "Mr. Cason, I finished everything. I will see you after school tomorrow."

Mr. Cason looked at him with a smile and said, "Have a good night."

Ben ran home. He had homework that needed to be done and dinner should be ready soon. He had worked up an appetite. On the walk home, he thought about what Mary had said about the job being saved for him. Reverend King, his pastor, had preached one time about what God has for you is for you. That no one can take away what God has in store for you. Even if it takes longer for you to find it or for you to be in the right position to receive it. Ben smiled and thanked God for the job that had been saved for him. As he turned down the street that led to his house, he saw David and Mary running toward him. He ran to meet them.

Mary declared, "Mom has cooked a great Sunday dinner: Roasted chicken, cabbage, and some cornbread dressing."

Ben said, "That sounds delicious. That's one of my favorite meals."

David interjected, "She let me help. I washed the dishes while she was cooking, so when I clean up after dinner, there won't be that much for me to clean. We also bought some bruised bananas that were reduced in price at the grocery store yesterday. Mom showed me how to make a banana pudding for dessert. I also learned that the riper the banana is the sweeter it is."

As they walked through the door, Ben rushed to his mother to give her a hug and kiss.

Mom said, "Dinner is ready, go wash up."

Ben hurried to the restroom. When he came out, everyone was seated at the table. It was Mom's turn to say grace. She blessed the food and asked God to continue to take care of her family and provide all that we need. Then she started her inquisitions.

She asked, "Mary, is anything special coming up this week?"

Mary said proudly, "Yes ma'am, I made my decision about a topic for the History Fair. It is 'Around the World in Eighty Days'. I plan to lay out how you can travel around the world, the countries you should visit, and some historical facts about each country. What do you think?"

Mom said, "That sounds interesting. Will it challenge you or is that just something easy?"

Mary said, "I can make it challenging, but you're right it will be somewhat easy. I will think of something else."

Mom stated firmly, "No, I don't want you to abandon the topic. I just want to make sure you are challenged. How much time do you have? I don't want you waiting until the last minute."

Mary said, "The project has to be completed by Thanksgiving, so that gives me two months."

Ben exclaimed, "Mom, this dinner is delicious; I love your roasted chicken and cornbread dressing."

With his mouth full of food David said, "Me too!"

Mom asked, "David, what do you have planned this week?"

David said proudly, "I've already planned the menu for the days I have to cook. I've done all of my home work for the week. These new teachers give students what they call a syllabus. It tells you what chapter will be covered each week and any homework assignments with due dates. We did not have syllabuses at our old school."

Ben added, "You're right. In some of my classes I have the same thing."

Mom asked, "Do you feel that the education you are receiving now from the school since you integrated, is better than what you were receiving before?"

Ben said, "I have noticed that the text books that we are using now were published more recently or new. Some of the books, I used last year at the black school, were ten years old. I still feel that my previous teachers taught me well. I think the information that I am being taught is just more current. Does that make any sense?"

Mom said, "Yes it does."

Ben continued, "I also noticed that the books we use now are thicker than the books we had at the black school. I saw some ninth-grade math books the other day. They had the same cover as the ninth-grade math book that I used last year at the black school, but this book had more pages. I skimmed through it and saw some concepts that I had never seen."

Mom said, "I know, I've heard stories that the white schools received not only newer books, but books that covered more information. In some counties the blacks had to pay for their books. When I was in school, some of our books were twenty years old. We were just happy to have a book. Some things like math and reading do not change, but history and science does. Well, that's one good thing that has come out of the integration of schools."

Mom looked at Ben and asked, "How was your work day?"

Ben smiled and replied, "It was good. Mr. Cason is really happy with my work. He told me that I was no longer on probation. The job is mine as long as I wanted it."

Mary interjected, "I thought you were on probation for ninety days, it's only been a week?"

Ben said proudly, "I was, but not anymore. He told me he was very pleased with my work."

Mom said, "That's great!"

Ben continued, "I found out Mr. Cason is eighty years old!"

David said, "Wow, I told you he was old, but I didn't think he was that old."

Ben said, "His wife died twenty years ago, he has no children or siblings. I think he is lonely. He really appreciated the lunch you made him yesterday, he brought it up again today."

Mom said, "I'm glad. You continue to be good to him. God wants us to not only respect our elders but take care of them. Since he does not have any family, I'm sure he enjoys when you are there."

Ben said, "I think so too. He smiles when I come in the shop and he seems sad when I have to go."

Wiping her mouth with the back of her hand, Mom said, "Let's continue to pray for Mr. Cason. God has brought him into our lives for a reason."

5

JEALOUSY IS REAL

It was a beautiful Saturday, the sun was shining bright, with a cool breeze indicating that the seasons were changing. Ben entered the door of the golf shop.

Mr. Cason smiled and said, "Hello Ben, it's a beautiful fall day here in Fairville."

Ben replied, "Yes sir, it is. The walk to work was very nice. It's not hot and the leaves are changing. I can't believe I have been working here for over two months."

Smiling Mr. Cason said, "That's right, you have done a great job on this place. My customers have commented how nice it looks in here. Everything is so organized, I can fill orders quicker, and customers don't have to wait long at all. I am so glad I hired you."

Ben smiled as he went into the restroom to make sure everything was clean. As he entered the storage room, he beamed with pride. The storage room looked great. It took a lot of work, but everything was labeled and in an organized system that he and Mr. Cason could follow. Ben had suggested that Mr. Cason create a 'marked down table' to sell some of the items that were old or not on the current inventory.

Later that day while working in the storage room, Ben heard Mr. Cason talking to a customer. He could see that it was a man with his son. Ben continued to busy himself in the storage room.

Mr. Cason said proudly, "Jerry, I ordered three cases of those yellow tees that you like. Would you like to buy some today?"

Jerry said, "Yes I would, I want two dozen. I love those tees. It makes it easier for me to see which tee is mine on the golf course. My color-blind condition is deuteranomaly. It makes yellow seem redder to me. So, I know which tee is mine. With everyone else having a white tee, my tee stands out."

Mr. Cason said with a loud voice, "Ben, please bring me the box of yellow tees!"

Ben quickly retrieved the yellow tees and handed them to Mr. Cason.

Ben smiled at the customers and went back into the storage room.

Jerry asked angrily, "Who is that colored boy?"

Mr. Cason replied, "That is Ben Davis, he works part-time for me."

Jerry asked seditiously, "If you needed help, why didn't you hire my son. He's seventeen now?"

Pointing at the window, Mr. Cason said calmly, "Jerry, I had a sign in that window for six months before I hired Ben. You come in this store at least three times a month. You pass by the store at least weekly going to the drug store. I can't imagine that you did not see the sign."

Jerry said, "Yeah, I saw the sign, but I kept forgetting to ask you about it. You should have said something to me, you knew I had a son! That way you would not have to hire that colored boy."

As nicely as he could Mr. Cason said, "Yes, I knew you had a son, but I did not know he was interested in working. You told me once, that you had a hard time getting him to take out the trash."

Jerry felt insulted, he said vehemently, "I don't want the tees. I will drive the hour and a half to Macon before I buy anything else from this store!"

Mr. Cason said, "I'm sorry that you feel that way Jerry, but if you change your mind. I am here!"

Jerry angrily pushed his teenage son out the door. The teenage son looked back at Mr. Cason with bitterness and rolled his eyes.

Ben ran into the front part of the store. He asked, "Mr. Cason, did I do something wrong?"

Mr. Cason smiled and said, "No Ben, you did nothing wrong. That man is Jerry Green, he is upset because I did not hire his son. I have no regrets in hiring you, so you have nothing to be worried about. Please put these tees back in the storage room."

Ben took the box of tees, then asked, "Mr. Cason didn't you say that these tees were only purchased by that man?"

Mr. Cason laughed and said, "Yes, that's true. I'm going to have to put them on the 'marked down' table. Maybe someone else will be interested in them."

Ben continued to busy himself with his work. He and Mr. Cason had lunch together. Mr. Cason brought in spam sandwiches with some barbeque potato chips. Ever since Ben shared his lunch with Mr. Cason on that first Saturday, they had alternated who would bring in lunch on Saturdays. Mr. Cason brought in some things that Ben had never eaten before, some were good, some were not.

Ben asked, "Mr. Cason have you noticed that the display case looks better each week?"

Mr. Cason laughed and said, "You are right. It is beautiful."

After finishing his lunch Mr. Cason said, "Ben, I have one more project I would like you to work on. Follow me!"

The phone rang, Mr. Cason answered, "Cason Golf Shop, may I help you?"

The person on the phone vehemently said, "You're going to regret who you hired!" Then hung up.

Mr. Cason said nothing, he just hung up the phone. He looked at Ben and said, "Ben, please follow me!"

Ben followed Mr. Cason out of the back door. Two trucks were behind the shop. They were filthy and covered with branches and debris.

Mr. Cason stated, "I would like you to wash these trucks. They work fine. They are only about two years old. The Ford dealership gave me a great deal, so I bought two. I don't know why. They have not been driven in a while. I want to start making deliveries to the golf course. Then I will be able to charge them a delivery fee. Today, if you can clean them up inside and out, I would appreciate it."

Ben replied, "Yes sir."

As Mr. Cason was walking back into the building, he looked back at Ben and asked, "Ben, do you know how to drive?"

Ben laughed and said, "No sir."

Mr. Cason asked, "Do you think your mom would mind if I taught you?"

Ben laughed and said, "I'm sure she won't mind, but I will ask her tonight."

Mr. Cason said, "Great! I picked up a motor vehicle instruction book that you can study to prepare for the driver's license test."

Ben was speechless.

Mr. Cason asked, "Are you OK?"

Ben replied, "Yes sir, I just never expected to learn to drive. We don't have a car and I know very few people with one."

Mr. Cason smiled and went back into the shop. Ben cleaned the trucks inside and out before he left for the day. They looked brand new.

The phone rang again, Mr. Cason answered, "Cason Golf Shop, how can I help you?"

The person on the other end said very nastily, "You're going to regret what you did?" Then there was a click.

Mr. Cason hung up the phone and pondered who could be calling him.

At the end of the day, Mr. Cason gave Ben the motor vehicle instruction book then said, "Start reading! We will have our first driving lesson tomorrow."

Ben smiled and said, "See you tomorrow, Mr. Cason."

Ben rushed home, he could not wait to tell his family. His siblings met him as soon as he turned down the street to go home. They had been doing that every day he worked. Sometimes if David was busy cooking, Mary would come by herself. They laughed as they ran home. Each day Miss Bessie would be looking out the window. They always waved.

As he entered the door, Ben stated, "Something smells delicious!"

David replied, "It's spaghetti with meat balls and green beans with red potatoes."

Ben asked, "David, did you cook this or Mom?"

Mom said, "It was all David. I learned a few things from him today."

David said, "This is one of the meals we cooked in Home Economics last week. When we went to the grocery store this morning, Mom let me buy a small package of ground beef. I took some canned beans, drained them, then smashed them up. I mixed it with the ground beef to stretch it. Then I was able to make more meatballs. I hope they taste good."

Mom said proudly, "David, I'm sure they are delicious. You're learning so much in that Home Economics class."

David said, "Yes ma'am. Everyone in class keeps coming over to my station to see what I'm doing. The Home Economics teacher is surprised at some of the things I make."

Everyone sat at the table. Mary could not wait to eat. She said grace somewhat quickly, Mom was not pleased. She gave Mary a look.

Then Mary said, "I don't taste the beans, it tastes good."

Mom tasted the spaghetti and meatballs, she stated, "David, the meatballs have a good texture. I can taste the beans, but they don't taste bad. Did you put some sugar in the sauce when I was not looking?"

David replied, "Yes ma'am just a little. It tones down the acidity of the tomato sauce."

Mom declared, "It's delicious!"

David said, "Mom, I didn't say anything earlier. However, for Christmas Mrs. Smith, the Home Economics teacher, said that we can bake cakes to sell if we like. We have to purchase all of the ingredients, but any money that we make we get to keep. We must cook the cakes afterschool in the classroom, but it will count as extra credit. I don't need the extra credit, but I want to do it. Maybe I can sell cakes as my part-time job."

Mom said, "Wow, who knew that Ben getting a job would be the catalyst that would bring such a multiple blessing. David's talent of cooking was revealed and now it could possibly bring more money in the house. I can't believe it."

Mary asked, "When are you going to cook a cake for us?"

David said, "I don't know, we need ingredients."

Ben said, "I will give you money for ingredients."

David beamed with joy and said, "Great, I will bake a cake next week."

Mom looked at Ben and said, "Ben, that's very generous of you. How was your day at work?"

Ben said, "It was great, Mr. Cason wants to teach me how to drive. He wants to know if it's OK with you?"

Mom put her fork down and asked, "Drive?"

Ben replied, "Yes ma'am, he has two trucks behind the shop. He wants to start making deliveries to the golf course. He wants to give me my first lesson tomorrow. He gave me this book to start studying for the driver's permit."

Mom said, "I think it's another blessing God has prepared for us."

Mary exclaimed, "This year is full of blessings."

Mom said, "Yes, it is and we have not come into the holiday season yet."

On the next day after Sunday School and church, Ben rushed to the golf shop for work. He got there earlier than usual, he found Mr. Cason talking to the deputy police. The big window of the shop had been broken, things were knocked down and broken in the shop. On the door was written in spray paint, '*You are gonna regret who you hired*'.

Ben went to the back room to access the damage. He heard Mr. Cason crying out to him, "Ben! Ben! I don't see the display case. They took the display case!"

Ben rushed into the front of the shop and said, "Mr. Cason it's OK. I had left it in the storage room. I was still polishing it yesterday."

Mr. Cason relaxed and said, "I'm so glad. Please look around so we can make a list of what has been taken and the damage that has been done."

Ben asked, "Mr. Cason does the police know who did this?"

Mr. Cason replied, "No, not yet. He started a report and said that he would stop by later for the list of missing items and damage."

Ben busied himself trying to clean up the place. There was broken glass everywhere. He cleaned it all up and made a list of the items that were broken or missing. There was only one missing item on the list.

Mr. Cason read the list, he asked, "Ben, are you sure this is all that has been taken?"

Ben replied, "Yes sir. I checked the inventory three times, but the three cases of yellow tees are the only things that are missing."

Mr. Cason shook his head and said, "Then I know who did this? It had to be Jerry's son."

Ben asked, "Why would he break into your store like this?"

Mr. Cason said, "His father was very upset that I had not hired him and he resented the fact that I would hire a colored boy over him."

Ben stared at Mr. Cason then asked, "Mr. Cason, do you need me to quit?"

Mr. Cason said, "Ben, that is so unselfish of you. I do not want you to quit. You have helped me more than you realize."

Mr. Cason continued, "I'm going to the police station and give them this list. I will be back. Please continue your work. If a customer comes, please take care of them. You know what to do."

Mr. Cason walked out the door and down the sidewalk. He was not upset about the damage to the store, he had insurance that would take care of it. He was upset that someone would target him because of Ben. Ben was the best thing that had happened to him since he met his wife. He wondered how can people be so narrow minded. Things were supposed to be getting better.

As he opened the door to the police station, the deputy invited him into his office. Mr. Cason gave him the list of missing items and damage report.

Deputy Jones asked, "Mr. Cason are you sure this is all that is missing?"

Mr. Cason replied proudly, "Yes, I have a good inventory system now, so it was easy to access what was missing."

Deputy Jones asked, "How many customers buy this item?"

Mr. Cason replied, "Only one, Jerry Green."

Mr. Cason told him about the incident that happen on yesterday and the phone calls he had received.

Deputy Jones asked, "Would you like to press charges against the young man?"

Mr. Cason said, "No, I don't want to press charges. I do want you to let his father, Jerry, know what happened."

Deputy Jones stated, "Mr. Cason, you have owned that golf shop since I was a little boy. I have noticed that since you hired that teenager, your shop has looked a lot better. I have heard other people talking about it several times."

Mr. Cason smiled and said proudly, "Yes, Ben Davis has done excellent work for me and I don't appreciate being threatened about hiring him. I don't want him bullied in any way. These harassing phone calls cannot become rife. They must stop!"

Deputy Jones smiled and said, "I will make sure I let Mr. Green and his son know that if anything else is done to your store or to Ben and his family, we will hold him responsible. I will also let him know that I plan to request an audit of his phone records to see if those calls originated from his home. I will put a good scare in them both. We have worked hard to get the high school under control since the integration at the start of the school year. There have not been any fights for over a month. We want Fairville to be a peaceful town."

Mr. Cason stood up and said, "I appreciate that. Thank you for your time."

Before Mr. Cason returned to the golf shop, he stopped by the hardware store to put an order in for a new window and some plywood to cover the broken window. He would pick up the plywood later. He also picked up some mineral spirits to remove the terrible message painted on the front door.

As Mr. Cason walked into the store, Ben was completing a sale. Ben walked the customer to the door as Mr. Cason always did and waved goodbye.

Mr. Cason said, "Ben, you demonstrated great customer service, you have learned well."

Ben said, "That's because I have a great teacher to emulate, one who is patient with me."

Mr. Cason laughed and said, "I picked up a few things from the hardware store. I will try to remove this paint from the glass in the door, you take care of everything else."

After Mr. Cason cleaned the window, he drove the truck to the hardware store to pick up the plywood. The truck smelled of disinfectant. It looked brand new. Surprisingly it cranked right up. He knew he needed to take it over to the auto shop for a tune up and to have it checked out completely.

When Mr. Cason returned from the hardware store with the plywood, he and Ben nailed it up.

Ben questioned, "Maybe we should write something on the plywood, so people will know that we are open?"

Mr. Cason said, "That's a good idea. There is some paint and a brush in the back. Paint on it: We are open."

Ben laughed and said, "That's to the point!"

After the wood was painted, it was time for the shop to close.

Mr. Cason said, "Ben, we did not get a chance today to have a driving lesson. We will get one in next weekend, keep studying so you will be ready."

Ben smiled and said, "Yes sir. I will see you after school tomorrow. Goodnight!"

Smiling Mr. Cason said, "I look forward to it."

Ben ran home, he had worked hard and was hungry. He was also getting in better shape, since he had to walk and sometimes run to and from work. As he turned down his street, there were his siblings waiting patiently for him.

They ran the rest of the way home. As they entered the door, Ben smelled fried chicken. He greeted his mother and hurried to wash up. It was his turn to say grace. He took his time and thanked God for the food, his protection, and continued blessing over his family and Mr. Cason.

Mom started her inquisitions and asked, "Mary, how are you coming with your entry for the History Fair? I can't wait to see it."

Mary said, "It's coming along. There are only two weeks before Thanksgiving and I'm almost finished. I stayed with my idea of 'Around the World in Eighty days'. I have made some three-dimensional items that represent the different countries that you should visit. I also have details about culture, food, climate, currency, and languages for each country. Did you know that in Japanese, some of their currency is called a Yen? I want to be a polyglot. My teacher says that the display is impressive."

Mom said, "That's great news. What is a polyglot?"

Mary said proudly, "It's someone who speaks different languages."

Mom exclaimed, "Wow, that's great. Have you learned a lot?"

Mary replied, "Yes ma'am, I know which countries I want to visit one day. I also made index cards with hello and goodbye in each language."

Mom said, "Wow, I can't wait to see it. David, what about you? Do you have anything special going on at school?"

David said, "Yes ma'am. Ben gave me the money I needed to buy the ingredients for the Holiday Cake Sale. I have signed up to bake ten cakes. My teacher, Mrs. Smith, helped me figure out how much I should charge for each cake. She also helped me developed a schedule of what cakes should be baked on which day. The Holiday Cake Sale will be on Saturday, December ninth. If I sell all ten of my cakes, I can make sixty-five dollars!"

Mary gasped and said, "That's a lot of money David!"

Mom said, "The same stipulations apply to you as they did to Ben regarding how your money is divided up. Remember the first ten percent goes to the church as tithes. You can give me thirty-five percent, you must save twenty-five percent and you get to use the other thirty percent as you please."

David exclaimed, "I remember! Mrs. Smith is also helping me make signs to advertise. She said I need a signup sheet just in case people want to place a future order. She also said that I should make a cake for people to sample. I'm so excited."

Mom smiled and said, "Mrs. Smith has been very helpful to you. I'm so glad. Let's make sure we pray for her just like we are praying for Mr. Cason. I'm also excited that God has revealed what one of your talents is. I know you have many more. He will reveal those too."

Mom looked at Ben and asked, "Ben, how was your day?"

Ben had just taken a bite of the delicious, crispy fried chicken, he swallowed and announced, "The golf shop was broken into last night."

Mary gasped, "Oh no!"

Ben said, "They broke the big window and wrote 'you're going to regret who you hired' on the glass door. Mr. Cason was very calm at first until he noticed that the display case was not in the front part of the shop. He started screaming Ben, Ben, they took the display case. I told him that the display case was safe in the storage room."

Mom said, "He cares a lot about that display case."

Ben said, "Yes ma'am, his father put it in the store in 1901. Now, he has it. It means a lot to him. I don't know if it's worth anything, but it has great sentimental value to Mr. Cason."

David asked, "Did the people who broke in take anything?"

Ben said, "The only things we found missing were three boxes of yellow tees."

Mary questioned, "What are yellow tees?"

Ben said, "A tee is a small plastic piece that golfers use to hold the golf ball before they swing at it. Yellow is the color. Most tees are white."

Mom said, "What they wrote on the window indicates they are mad at Mr. Cason for hiring you."

Ben said, "Mr. Cason told me not to worry about my job. He went down to the police station to talk to the deputy. He did not tell me what they said."

Mom bowed her head and prayed, "God we thank you for your hedge of protection around our family and Mr. Cason. We ask that you continue to take care of us and we thank you for all the doors you are opening and opportunities you are creating for our family. In Jesus name we pray. Amen."

Everyone said, "Amen."

David asked, "Do you think those people will come back?"

Ben said, "I don't know. Mr. Cason is not worried. We sealed up the window with plywood and cleaned the paint off of the door."

Mom said, "Let's continue to keep Mr. Cason in our prayers. I want us all to pray for whoever broke into the golf shop too. They have issues that only Jesus can heal. I'm very proud of each of you. You are all doing well in school. You are developing into responsible individuals. I could not be prouder. Let's finish this delicious meal before it gets cold."

David announced, "I've already finished!"

Everyone laughed.

6

HOLIDAY SEASON

It was now December and the Christmas season was approaching. The temperature was dropping, making every day colder. Mary won first prize at the History Fair. She was given a certificate and twenty-five dollars in cash. She received an automatic entry into the regional History Fair which is in March, the prize would be fifty dollars. If she does well there, her project will be entered into the State History Fair in May. The grand prize will be one hundred dollars.

Ben had been working with Mr. Cason for almost four months now. He had saved a lot of his money, however, he wanted to make a purchase today. Christmas was only seventeen days away.

As he entered the store, Ben kept rubbing his arms to warm up while shivering he said, "Mr. Cason, I noticed that all of your customers are white. Would you sell items to someone that is not white?"

Mr. Cason said laughingly, "Ben, you know the answer to that. Yes, I would. If they have money, they can purchase anything in my store."

Ben said, "I would like to make a purchase?"

Mr. Cason smiled and said, "Well then go shopping, I will check you out when you are ready!"

Ben went to the table that had the marked down items on it. He picked up some golf club tags and two drawstring bags with the Callaway logo on it. Calloway was a popular golf vendor.

He approached the counter, Mr. Cason asked, "Did you find everything you need?"

Ben said, "Yes sir I did. I want to give this bag to my mom for Christmas. People at the factory are always picking up her work bag by mistake. I will write her name on this golf club tag and put it on the drawstring bag. I think she will like it. The second one I will keep as my work bag."

Ben continued, "Since I have been working here, I have been able to help out with the bills, pay tithes, and even save some money."

Mr. Cason said, "Ben, I forgot to tell you one other benefit you are entitled to. You get a ten percent discount on items purchased in the shop."

Ben smiled and said, "That is great."

Mr. Cason said, "I wish I had more things you could purchase."

Ben said laughingly, "That's OK, I will keep my eyes open. You never know what I might see."

Mr. Cason finished the transaction and gave Ben his change. Ben put the money in the front pocket of his blue jeans.

Mr. Cason asked, "Ben, what do you keep the money you are saving in?"

Ben said, "I have an old coffee can."

Mr. Cason asked, "Do you want to open a bank account?"

Ben said, "I don't think blacks can open an account at the local bank!"

Mr. Cason said, "That's unconscionable! I will check into it and let you know."

Ben said, "Thank you!"

He took his items into the storage room and began working.

Mr. Cason entered the storage room and stated, "Ben, I reserved a seat for you to take the driver's license permit test on Tuesday. When you pass this test, you can drive the truck. However, you still have to have a licensed driver in the truck. In twelve months, you can take the road test. When you pass that, you will be able to drive by yourself."

Ben stopped working and looked at Mr. Cason, then said, "Mr. Cason, I'm ready for that test. I have read that book from cover to cover three times. I have memorized all of the road signs too."

Mr. Cason said, "That's great. I'm sure you will do well."

After work Ben rushed home. He was excited about everything. As he walked he prayed and thanked God for all the things he could think of. He was doing well in school. He had a part-time job. He had money saved. He would be able to purchase Christmas gifts for his family. In past years, he made arts and crafts gifts.

Ben turned down his street and no one was there to meet him. He knew something was wrong. He ran all of the way home. When he entered the door, he saw his mother sitting on the sofa, Mary and David were sitting next to her. He ran and kneeled at her feet.

He asked, "Mom, what's wrong?"

Mom said, "I have not been feeling well. I took half a day off from work and went to the doctor today. He said that I have hypertension, most people call it high blood pressure. This is not fatal. I just have to take medication. I'm not overweight and I walk every day. He said that I will be fine."

Ben asked, "OK, is there anything we can do to help."

Mom said, "I have to watch how much salt I eat. He wants me to go to the drug store every week; they will measure my blood pressure for me. So, I am well. Right now, I'm just a little tired and I have a headache. He said that is expected until my blood pressure lowers. Tomorrow is Saturday, so I can take it easy over the weekend and get ready for work on Monday."

Ben said, "Mom, we will help more."

Mom laughed and said, "You all do everything already."

Mary said, "We can do more, I can go to the laundry mat and wash the clothes."

Mom said, "You're only ten. You can't go to the laundry mat by yourself, but you can go with me. How is that?"

Mary smiled.

David said, "My Holiday Bake sale is tomorrow. I can go by myself. You don't have to go."

Mom exclaimed, "There is no way I'm missing that. I want to see all of the cakes you have baked. I want to hear everyone say how delicious your samples are. I will be fine. I have been bragging to my coworkers about what a good cook you are. Now, I will be able to tell them how great a baker you are too! What is that smell coming from the kitchen? It smells delicious?"

David said, "I made some soup. We had some leftover chicken in the refrigerator, so I made soup."

Mom said, "Let me go to the restroom, then I will be ready to eat!"

When Mom left the room, Mary pulled her brothers to the kitchen and said, "I have never seen Mom sick. She looks wan."

Ben agreed, "Me neither, let's just make sure we do all that we can. So, all she has to do is rest."

David said, "OK, I will cook dinner on the weekends too."

Mary said, "OK, let's pray that God will heal Mom."

Mom entered the room and saw the children talking.

She said, "I know you all are worried. Let's give our cares to the Lord and continue to live."

Everyone sat at the table. It was Mary's turn to say grace.

She prayed, "God, we come to you right now concerned about our mother. We give you these cares. We trust you God. We thank you for this food that we are about to receive. In Jesus name we pray, Amen."

Everyone said, "Amen."

As David filled everyone's bowl with soup, Mom started her inquisitions.

She asked, "Mary, how is school?"

Mary said, "Some of the students are being mean to me since I won the History Fair."

Mom asked, "Mean how?"

Mary said sadly, "They are saying things like, 'She thinks she is so smart'. They use to talk to me in class. Now they are not talking to me at all. I feel ostracized. The teacher told me not to worry about it. However, it does hurt my feelings."

Mom said, "Your teacher is right, it's those other kid's problem not yours. They will get tired of being mean to you soon. Then they will want you on their team or ask you your opinion. I know that your feelings are hurt now. Just like you said in that beautiful prayer about casting our cares on the Lord, you continue to cast your cares about this on the Lord too."

Mom continued, "In a way, they are trying to bully you. They say those hurtful things hoping you will change and not be smart. I will pray for them. God has made you very intelligent. That's one of your talents. Don't be embarrassed about how smart you are. It's a gift. Hold your head up high, don't be embarrassed. Those other kids wish they were as smart as you. You continue to work hard and show them how smart you really are! Yes, these kids are talking about you now, but one day God will send other people to celebrate you. Celebrate how smart you really are!"

Looking at David, Mom said, "David, this soup is delicious. God has given you a gift too. You have a talent for making good food. Do you have any goals that you've set?"

David said, "Yes ma'am. I was researching hypertension in the library. I wanted to know what I could do to make my cooking healthier. While I was there, I saw a book about culinary school?"

Mary said excitedly, "I know that word, it's cooking school!"

David said, "That's right. I know I'm only in the eighth grade, but right now I would love to go culinary school. It's very expensive."

Ben stated, "I was concerned about college expenses. A few years ago, Mr. Knowlton was a guest speaker at the black school. He said that there are federal grants, scholarships, and loans that are available to pay for college and vocational schools. He said, money is not a reason to say that you cannot get an education. He said come see him during your junior year of high school that he would help anyone apply for ways to pay for college. He said concentrate on learning as much as you can now, don't worry about the costs."

David said, "That's great news! I feel better."

Mom said, "Mr. Knowlton is right. I heard other parents talking about how he helped their children received grants.

He's a very nice man, I'm glad that he is willing to help you apply. I don't know anything about that."

Everyone laughed.

Mom said, "David, I will include culinary school in my prayer for you. God said, we have not because we ask not. So, let's make sure we ask God for what we need."

Mom looked at Ben and asked, "Sweetheart, how is school going for you?"

Ben said, "I'm doing well in all of my classes. It seems like since I've been working, I'm doing better in my classes. Mr. Cason is teaching me so many things. Some of my teachers bring up the same subjects, so I grasp the concepts much quicker, because I have seen them in action at the shop."

Mom said, "That's great."

Ben continued, "Mr. Cason made a reservation for me to take the driver's permit test on next Tuesday. I'm ready."

Mom said, "I know you are, I've seen you reading that book. It's worn out from you reading it so much."

Everyone laughed.

Mom said, "Ben, please ask Mr. Cason how much it costs to take the test. I don't want you to assume he is paying for it. If he offers that's fine, but if he doesn't; I want you to pay for it!"

Ben said, "Yes ma'am!"

Mom said, "Christmas is only a week or so away. Invite Mr. Cason to Christmas Dinner. You said that he did not have any family. David and I have a big meal planned."

Ben said, "I will. I think he will like that!"

Mary said, "I'm already thinking about what gifts I can give."

David said, "I have a list of different things, it will depend on how much money I make tomorrow at the bake sale."

Mom said, "I don't want you all to spend a lot of money on gifts. The gifts you made over the years have been very special to me."

Ben said, "I know, but this is the first year we have had money to spend."

Everyone laughed.

7

CHRISTMAS CELEBRATION

David sold all of his cakes at the bake sale. He made ninety dollars. His cakes were in such demand that some people paid more. Mom was doing well. The medication seemed to be working to regulate her blood pressure. Mr. Cason was very thankful for the invitation to Christmas dinner. David had orders for twenty Christmas cakes. He created a schedule for customers to pick up their cakes at the house, since school would be out.

On the Saturday before Christmas, Ben asked Mr. Cason, "We will be out of school for two weeks, would you like for me to work more during the break?"

Mr. Cason said, "Ben, I would love to spend more time with you, but I think that we should keep the regular schedule. I want you to have some time off from school during your break to rest. However, this summer, I would like for you to work forty hours a week. What do you think?"

Ben smiled and said, "That sounds great sir! Remember, Christmas dinner will be at three o'clock. I live at 605 Washington Drive, it's not far from here. It's a small blue house. It's right behind the middle school. The school that was the black school."

Mr. Cason said, "I know that area. Do I need to bring anything?"

Ben said, "Bring your appetite and some containers to take food home. My mom and David are planning a big meal."

Ben went back to work. Customers came in and out of the store. At lunchtime Ben pulled out his thermos and two bowls from his work bag. He gave Mr. Cason some soup that David made with some saltine crackers and a few cookies.

Mr. Cason tasted the soup, he said, "Ben, this soup is delicious! It has a great flavor and is very hearty. I see beans, carrots, chicken, and rice."

Ben proudly said, "My brother, David, made the soup. He wants to go to culinary school. He's only been cooking since I got this job. This is his second time making soup."

Surprised Mr. Cason said, "Really? I can see why he wants to go to culinary school. There is one in Atlanta at the Art Institute about two hours away."

Ben said, "We did not know that. I will tell David."

Mr. Cason asked, "Ben, can you cook this well?"

Ben laughed and said, "No sir, I have been cooking for about four years, but all I can do is fix a meal some better than others. I was never really interested in cooking like David. He definitely takes after my mom. She is a great cook."

Mr. Cason asked, "Will you have any problems getting over to the court house to take the driver's test on Tuesday?"

Ben said, "No sir, school is out so I can go over early. I read in the paper that the test is administered at nine o'clock in the morning, so I will be there early. Mr. Cason, do you know how much the test costs? I want to make sure I take enough money with me."

Mr. Cason replied, "I have already paid for your test when I made the reservation. So, all you have to do is show up and pass the test."

Ben said, "Sir, that's very generous. I can pay you back."

Mr. Cason smiled and said, "That is very nice of you to offer. You getting your driver's license benefits me just as much as it benefits you. So, I see it as paying for training for one of my employees."

Ben inquired, "Mr. Cason, how many employees have you had?"

Mr. Cason said, "Over the years I have had many. Some were teenagers like you. Other employees were adults. Some good, a few were bad. I had to let them go. None have been as excellent and tenacious of a worker as you. You are not only a hard worker, but intelligent, honest, and considerate. Those are qualities that will make you successful in everything you do."

Ben smiled and said, "I thought those traits were normal. They are required if you are a child of Phyllis Davis."

Mr. Cason laughed very loudly and said, "Unfortunately, your mom has not raised everyone else."

On Tuesday, Ben took the driver's permit test. When he received his learner's permit, he ran to Mr. Cason's shop.

He said, "Mr. Cason, Mr. Cason, I passed my test. Please, look at my picture!"

Mr. Cason smiled and said, "Ben, that's a great picture. You look winsome. I knew you would pass. I'm very proud of you. After Christmas we'll schedule regular driving lessons so you will be ready for your road test."

Mr. Cason asked, "What are you going to do the rest of the day since you don't have to come to work?"

Ben said, "I want to buy some Christmas gifts. I want to get a dictionary for Mary and some pretty bows for her hair.

I want to get David a *Betty Crocker Recipe Book*. I also want to pick up my mom one more thing, I'm not sure what. I figured I can get everything from the Dime Store or Maxwell's."

Mr. Cason said, "Well, you enjoy your day, I will see you tomorrow at three o'clock."

Ben proudly left the shop and went shopping. He still needed to get Mr. Cason something special for Christmas. What do you buy a man that is eighty years old and has everything he needs?

As he walked through the Dime Store, the cashier followed him down every aisle watching to see if he would steal anything. That was the regular routine whenever a black person came into the store. Despite her foot steps behind him, Ben thought about Mr. Cason. He had never seen or heard Mr. Cason talk about liquor, smoking, or chewing tobacco. He seemed to be healthy. He lived alone. Then he saw the perfect gift. It cost a little more than he had anticipated, but Mr. Cason was worth it. The week went by fast. Christmas was on a Monday. David finished all of his cake orders, he made over one hundred and fifty dollars.

On Christmas Eve there was no real tradition, everyone sat around the Christmas tree and talked until they got tired. There was a small artificial tree that was about four feet tall. It had very few decorations, but it was beautiful when the lights were turned on. Christmas music could be heard on the radio. Mom and David had been busy all weekend prepping or cooking food. So, it did not take long for everyone to say goodnight.

On Christmas morning Mary woke up first as usual. Our tradition was to read the Christmas story and exchanged gifts before breakfast.

Mom said happily, "OK everyone, it's time to read the Christmas story."

Mary retrieved the Bible and passed it to Ben to read. He started reading Luke Chapter Two. When he finished, Mary was there to pass out the gifts. Mom was overwhelmed, she had so many gifts at her feet.

Mary said, "Open mine first please."

Mom smiled and asked, "Which one is yours? There are so many."

Mary passed Mom the gift wrapped in blue paper. Blue was Mom's favorite color. Mom unwrapped the gift trying to save the beautiful paper.

As she opened the box, she exclaimed, "Mary, this is beautiful. Where did you buy this?"

Mary said proudly, "You remember the field trip to the museum in Macon we took after Thanksgiving. The museum had a gift shop, I took my share of the money from the History Fair and bought all of my Christmas gifts. Do you like it?"

Holding up the gift, Mom exclaimed, "This is a beautiful handkerchief with lace trim. I will carry it to church in my purse. Thank you so much Mary."

Mary beamed with joy.

David passed Mom a gift and said, "Please open mine next."

It was not wrapped in gift paper, but the box was taped shut.

David said, "I didn't wrap it because I knew you would open it slowly."

Everyone laughed.

Mom took her sharp fingernails and broke the seal on the tape.

She opened the box and gasped, "David, this is so nice."

As she held up a beautiful blue shawl, she stood up for everyone to see.

David said, "Well, with the money I made from the cakes, I went to Maxwell's Store in town. I told Mr. Maxwell that I wanted something very nice for my mom. He showed me a few things, but nothing was nice enough. Some were even tawdry. Then he showed me this shawl. I saw that it was blue and knew you would like it."

Mom modeled the shawl, walking around the living room with her shawl and waving her handkerchief.

Ben stated, "Mom, I have a few gifts for you. Please open this one first."

Mom tried to open the gift a little quicker, but she could not bring herself to tear the paper.

Ben laughed and said, "Next year, I'm using tape like David did."

Everyone laughed.

Mom finally got the box open. It was a new purse.

Mom exclaimed, "I needed a new purse, I love it! It has an adjustable strap. Thank you so much Ben. I can't wait to carry it to church and to the grocery store."

Mom paraded around the living room with her shawl and purse with her handkerchief in her hand. She was so happy.

Ben said lovingly, "Mom, please sit down, I have one more gift for you."

Everyone patiently waited for her to open her last gift. As she pulled out the Calloway drawstring bag with the name tag already attached, she started to cry.

Ben, David, and Mary all leaned over and hugged their mother.

Wiping her tears with the back of her hand, Mom said, "Ben, thank you so much. No one is going to take my work bag now. If they do, they will see my name on it. Thank you so much."

Ben laughed and said, "I thought the same thing. I bought me one too, so don't you take mine!"

Everyone laughed.

Mom said, "OK now it's time for me to lavish you all with gifts."

Mary said, "Lavish, that means to give freely!"

Everyone laughed.

Mom passed out one gift to each child. As they each tried to open their gifts carefully, Mom relished in the sight of her beautiful children. She prayed silently and thanked God for her health and her children.

Mary exclaimed, "Mom, this is beautiful."

Mary stood up to show off her new pink shoulder bag and black patent leather shoes.

She exclaimed, "I can't wait to wear my new shoes to church. Can I carry my purse to school?"

Mom said, "Yes you can. I think you are responsible enough to keep up with it."

David finished opening his gift, he gasped, "Mom, this is awesome. I know this was expensive. You didn't have to do this."

David held up a set of four chef knives.

Mom said, "I got a great deal at the Western Auto store. They have some cooking accessories in the front part of the store now. These were a great deal. So, don't you worry about what they cost!"

David said, "Every chef needs good knives! Thank you, Mom. I love you!"

Ben finally opened his gift, he was speechless. He held up a leather wallet. It had a place for his identification card and a secret compartment.

He exclaimed, "Mom, this is genuine leather. David! Mary feel how soft it is."

As his siblings passed the wallet around, Ben said, "Mom, you always know exactly what we need. Thank you so much."

Mom said, "You all have inherited that sense too. I'm so glad that you like your gifts."

Mary announced, "I have something for David and Ben too."

She passed them her gifts and waited patiently for them to open them.

Ben opened his gift first, it was a journal with the logo of the museum on it.

Mary said, "I figured you could write down your goals and dreams in it."

David opened his gift, it was a journal with the logo of the museum on it.

Mary said, "I figured you could write down recipes and stuff in it."

Everyone laughed.

Ben said, "I love it. Thanks Mary."

David said, "I love it too. Thanks Mary."

David passed out his gifts for Ben and Mary. Mary rushed to open hers. She held up an atlas. It was a very large bound book with hundreds of pages of maps of different countries and cities."

David said, "My history teacher was clearing out his storage room. He put a lot of books on the table and told us we could take whatever we liked. I saw the atlas and thought of you."

Jumping up and down, Mary screamed, "I love it. I love it. Thanks David."

Ben opened his gift, it was a set of gloves.

David said, "I know your hands have been cold when you walked home, especially since you out grew your warm coat and Mom gave it to me. I could not buy you a coat but I thought you would appreciate the gloves."

Ben said, "I do appreciate the gloves. Yes, it has been chilly, but that just makes me walk faster. Thank you, David."

Everyone laughed.

Mom said, "Ben, I know you need a coat. I have one on layaway for you. Hopefully I will finish paying for it soon."

Ben smiled and said, "Mom, I'm fine. The weather has not been that cold!"

Ben passed out his gifts to David and Mary. Mary rushed to unwrapped her gift. It was a big dictionary and a large assortment of hair accessories.

Mary gasped, "I love it! This is the new unabridged dictionary printed just last year. Oh! Mom look at all of the hair accessories. I have bows in every color. Look some headbands too. Thank you so much Ben. Thank you so much."

David opened his gift to find the *Betty Crocker Cook Book*. David asked, "Did you get this at the Dime Store?"

Ben said, "Yes!"

David said, "I saw it and wanted it. However, I knew I could not buy it right now. I wanted to buy all of my Christmas gifts first. I really did want it. Thank you so much Ben."

Mary said, "There is one more gift under the tree."

Ben said, "That's for Mr. Cason. I got him a gift."

Mom said, "That was very nice of you Ben. OK, let's eat breakfast. We're having pancakes and sausage."

Mary, Ben, and David cleaned up the trash while Mom cooked breakfast. The morning flew by David and Mom busied themselves in the kitchen preparing dinner. There was a knock at the door at exactly 3:00 pm. Ben opened the door to let Mr. Cason in. As he opened the door, Mr. Cason was holding a fruit basket and a big gift box.

Ben smiled and said, "Mr. Cason, please come in, let me help you."

Mr. Cason smiled and said, "Merry Christmas!"

Mom rushed into the room, Ben introduced Mr. Cason to his mother, brother, and sister.

Mr. Cason said, "I am so happy to meet you all. I feel like I know you, Ben talks about you all the time."

Mr. Cason took the big fruit basket from Ben and gave it to Mom, then said, "This is for you and your family. Thank you so much for inviting me to dinner."

Mom took the big fruit basket and said, "Oh, this is the largest fruit basket I have ever seen. Thank you so much."

Mom put the basket on the coffee table, then said, "Dinner will be ready soon, please have a seat."

Mom and David rushed back into the kitchen. Mary said, "Mr. Cason, I am glad that you are here. Ben talks about you all the time too."

Mr. Cason smiled while taking a seat and holding the gift box.

Mary asked, "Who is that gift for?"

Mr. Cason said, "Thank you Mary, I forgot I was holding it. Ben, this is for you, Merry Christmas."

Mary screamed, "Mom, David, Mr. Cason gave Ben a gift!"

Mom and David rushed back into the room. Ben took the gift and sat down to open it.

Ben said, "Thank you Mr. Cason! You did not have to get me anything. I got you a little something too."

Ben reached under the tree to retrieve the gift. He gave it to Mr. Cason.

Mr. Cason said, "Oh my, I did not expect anything. You are so thoughtful."

Mary suggested excitedly, "You can open them together."

Ben opened his gift first, he pulled out a black coat.

Ben said, "Mr. Cason, this is too expensive."

Mom said, "Ben is right; we can't accept this."

Mr. Cason said, "Oh! Please accept it. I know Ben had to pass down his coat to David. This coat is for him just as much as it is for me. I don't want him to get sick and miss work."

Everyone laughed.

Mom said, "Well, if you put it like that. Ben you can keep it."

Ben put the coat on and said, "It fits perfectly. The sleeves are long enough and it's so warm. Oh look, it has a hood too. Thank you very much Mr. Cason."

Mary exclaimed, "Mr. Cason, please finish opening your gift."

Mr. Cason said, "OK Mary! Ben is right you are loquacious."

Mary smiled and said, "I know, I can be talkative and importunate too."

Mr. Cason laughed and said, "What does that mean?"

Mary smiled and said, "Persistent. I apologize. Now, please open your gift!"

Mr. Cason laughed out loud. As he opened the gift, he thought about the last time he received a Christmas gift. It had been many years. He took his time, enjoying every moment. Finally, he was finished and as he opened the box he put his hands over his mouth and smiled.

Mary screamed, "What did you get? What did you get?"

Mr. Cason said, "It is a beautiful frame with a picture of me and my wife standing in front of the golf shop. This picture was taken many years ago. I thought that I had lost it."

Ben said, "When I was cleaning up the storage room. I came across this picture and some other keepsakes in one of the boxes. I created a cache and put them all in one of the bins just in case you asked about them. When you didn't, I thought it would be nice to put the picture in a new frame."

Mr. Cason said, "This is a wonderful gift Ben. So thoughtful. I'm trying not to cry, but I can't help it."

Mr. Cason pulled his handkerchief out of his pocket to wipe his tears. He stood up and gave Ben a hug. Ben was so happy that he liked the gift.

Mom said, "Ben, that was a great gift. OK, it's time for dinner. Everyone please be seated."

The dinner was delicious. Mr. Cason ate until he could not move. After dinner Mom packed up leftovers for Mr. Cason to take home. We all sat around the tree and talked until it was dark. It was the best Christmas ever.

8

TIME GOES BY

Ben continued to work at the store, David continued to market his cake baking business, and Mary won the state History Fair. Mom was healthy and happy. All of the bills were paid and she was able to buy some of the things she needed or wanted for the house. Mr. Cason celebrated every holiday and birthday with the Davis' family.

Mr. Cason gave Ben driving lessons. Ben got his driver's license in December 1973. The school years seem to go by fast now that he was working. David was able to take another Home Economics class when he entered high school. Mary seemed to get even smarter now that she was in middle school. She was determined to improve her lexicon.

Time went by so fast, it was now Ben's senior year of high school. Mr. Knowlton helped Ben complete the grant forms. He applied for admission to colleges. There were five colleges in Macon, which was an hour and a half away from Fairville. Three of the colleges were private, so Ben knew not to apply to them. Even though it was 1974, a lot of things had not changed racially.

Ben was accepted into Middle Georgia State University. He then applied for academic scholarships. Mom and Mr. Cason were very proud of him. It was now January 1975 Ben was working hard in the store.

Mr. Cason asked, "Ben, have you heard anything from the college about the scholarship?"

Ben said, "No sir, not yet. I asked Mr. Knowlton if I should be worried. He said no. The deadline for scholarship applications just ended and it would take possibly another month before I heard a reply."

Mr. Cason asked, "What is your plan B? You should always have a backup plan!"

Ben said, "Mr. Knowlton said, I should receive enough federal grant money to pay for the tuition, but that staying in the dorm was not cheap. So, if I got the scholarship, it would pay for tuition and my grant money could pay for housing. Mr. Knowlton said that if I do not get the scholarship, that I could apply for a student loan."

Mr. Cason asked, "Ben, did you ever tell me what you plan to study? I'm getting older now, I don't remember if you did."

Ben laughed and said, "No Mr. Cason, I really just made a decision. I have decided to study business. Since I have been under your tutelage, I have learned so much. I really enjoy this work."

Mr. Cason chuckled and said, "That's great, you will make a great businessman."

Ben said, "It was somewhat of an easy decision. I'm not interested in medicine or engineering. I'm not an artist. I did not want to be a teacher, so business seemed like a good choice."

Mr. Cason said, "I'm very proud of you Ben. You have made my latter years pure joy."

Ben smiled and said, "Mr. Cason I never told you this, but when I got this job. Mary said, that since no one else had applied for the job, it was like it was saved for me."

Mr. Cason said, "Mary is very insightful, I think she's right. I was wondering why in six months no one had even asked me about the job. I figured the right person would come along and you did."

Ben said, "Sir, I have loaded the truck with the supplies for the golf course. Do you need anything while I'm there?"

Mr. Cason said, "No I don't. When you get back, I want you to go to the court house with me."

Ben said, "Yes sir, see you soon!"

Mr. Cason grabbed the phone to call Hank Jennings. Hank Jennings was one of the two lawyers in Fairville.

Mr. Cason asked, "Hank, do you have time for me to come by and sign those papers today?"

Hank Jennings replied, "Yes Mr. Cason, I will be in my office until two o'clock."

Mr. Cason said, "That is great, I will stop by in about an hour."

When Ben returned from the golf course, he entered the shop through the back door. He saw a customer come through the front door, so he busied himself with things in the storage room.

Mr. Cason said, "Hello Jerry! It is nice to see you."

Jerry said, "Hello Charlie! I was wondering if you had any more of those yellow tees."

Mr. Cason said, "No Jerry! I don't, but I can order you some."

Jerry said, "I would appreciate that."

Mr. Cason asked, "Is there anything else you need?"

Jerry said slowly, "Yes, I would like to apologize for what

happened a couple of years ago. I'm sorry. For the last two years, I have had to get my son out of so much trouble. He has committed so many malfeasances. Some I was able to refute, even though I knew that he was guilty. I finally realized that it all started two years ago, when I failed to correct him when he vandalized your store and stole from you."

Mr. Cason said, "I am sorry that you have had problems with your son. I heard that he recently got in trouble in Macon during the summer."

Jerry said sadly, "Yes, he did. This time I won't be able to help him. He robbed a grocery store at gun point. He has gotten mixed up with illegal drugs. It's a big mess. He has become a sybarite. If I had just corrected him two years ago, instead I thanked him for the yellow tees he stole from you. I was jealous that the Davis' boy was a better worker than my son."

Mr. Cason said, "We all make mistakes. I hope that your son straightens up and the court goes easy on him."

Jerry said, "Thank you. I understand that young man that's working for you will be going to Middle Georgia State University in Macon. That's a good school."

Mr. Cason said proudly, "Yes he will. We are waiting to hear if he will receive an academic scholarship."

With deep conviction Jerry said, "I wish him the best. I was wrong to speak negatively about him. I know that I vilified him to other people. I've learned a lot over the last few years. I used to be so sanctimonious! I am so sorry!"

Mr. Cason smiled and said, "Those yellow tees should be in next Tuesday. Please stop by."

Jerry said, "I will see you then. Bye Charlie."

He then turned to walk out of the door.

Ben entered the front part of the store and said, "I'm sorry that his son is in trouble."

Mr. Cason laughed and said, "I told you that Phyllis Davis needs to raise everybody. Are you ready to go to the courthouse?"

Ben said, "Yes sir. Let me lock the back door."

As they walked through town to the courthouse, Mr. Cason said, "Ben, this is a nice town to live in. I know it's small, but overall, it's very nice. I sense that it is changing for the better."

Ben said, "I know. I'm excited about going to college in Macon, but I will miss Fairville."

As they entered the front door of the courthouse, Mr. Cason greeted everyone nicely. Mr. Hank Jennings was standing in the hallway.

He said very friendly, "Mr. Cason, Ben, I am glad to see you two."

Ben thought how does he know my name.

Mr. Jennings opened his office door and pointed to two seats then said, "Please have a seat."

Ben waited for Mr. Cason to take the first seat.

Mr. Cason said, "Thank you so much Hank for getting all of the paper work in order for me."

Mr. Jennings said, "No problem Mr. Cason, I am happy to do it."

Ben sat silently, but was wondering what paperwork.

Mr. Jennings asked, "Ben, do you have your identification with you?"

Ben replied, "Yes sir."

He stood up to access his wallet, then he gave his driver's license to Mr. Jennings and sat back down.

Mr. Cason turned to Ben and said, "Ben, I don't know if you noticed, but I am getting a little slower these days. I will be eighty-three on my birthday."

Ben smiled.

Mr. Cason expounded, "You know I don't have any children. So, when something happens to me, I need someone I can turn everything over too. I don't have much, but I want to turn it over to you."

Ben whined, "Me? Mr. Cason?"

Mr. Cason said, "Yes, you. I know I can trust you. So, Hank has drawn up these papers that he needs you to sign."

Ben was holding back his tears.

Then with sincere appreciation he said, "Mr. Cason you know I would do anything for you. You know how this town is!"

Mr. Cason said, "Yes, I know. That is why I have asked Hank to make sure everything is legal and in order. Don't you worry about a thing. This town is changing for the better. I know there are still some hidden racial issues. This is what I want."

Ben said, "Mr. Cason, I know you have taught me a lot, but I feel so unprepared."

Mr. Cason said, "I have a few more years left in me. This business degree, that you are pursuing, will continue to prepare you better than I ever could."

Mr. Jennings passed Ben several documents that required his signature. Ben signed on the lines that were indicated. Mr. Jennings reviewed all of the documents to make sure everything was in order and gave Ben back his identification.

Mr. Cason looked at Ben and said, "I love your family, but right now I want you to keep this a secret. This is paramount. I need time for this town to change a little more."

Ben said, "Yes, sir."

Mr. Cason stood up and shook Mr. Jennings hand.

Mr. Jennings smiled at Ben and said, "I heard that you are going to Middle Georgia State University. I graduated from there many years ago. You will enjoy it. In the future if you need anything, don't hesitate to come to me. Please consider me one of your allies."

Ben smiled and said, "Thank you!"

As they walked back to the golf shop, Ben was silent.

Mr. Cason said, "Son, don't fret. Everything is going to be alright."

Ben worked the rest of the day like nothing happened. He started paying more attention to Mr. Cason, he was getting slower. That only made him work harder to make sure everything was in place and taken care of.

On Saturday, February 15, 1975, Ben received a letter from Middle Georgia State University in the mail. Mom, David, and Mary were all anxious wondering what the letter said. Ben took a deep breath and opened the letter. Ben read the letter silently and quickly.

Mary exclaimed, "Read it aloud, don't keep us waiting!"

Ben smiled and said, "It says that I have been awarded an academic scholarship that includes tuition, books, housing, and meals as long as I maintain a 3.0 average. Scholarship does not negate any grants that I may receive. If I accept this scholarship, I have to sign and mail back this document before March 15, 1975."

Mary asked, "What is a 3.0?"

Ben explained, "I think that is college lingo for a B. I have to ask Mr. Knowlton to make sure."

David said, "Then that is not a problem, you're an A student."

Mom was wiping her tears with the back and front of her hand, she said, "Ben this is what I have been praying for. What you have been working so hard for. God has come through for us. You will be the first person in our family to go to college, but not the last! God has plans for the rest of you too!"

Ben said, "Yes ma'am I know. I feel overwhelmed."

Mom said, "I know, but God has blessed you because not only who you are, but who he expects you to be. I know that is a heavy burden, but he has prepared you for this. Walk with your head up and continue to do your best."

Ben said, "Mom, suppose I get there and I can't do it."

Mom said, "Erase that thought from your mind. Even when things get hard and I know they will. Always remember that you can do all things through Christ. You are resilient. If God gave it to you, he will bring you through it."

Everyone hugged each other and celebrated. The next day Ben showed Mr. Cason the letter. Mr. Cason read the letter out loud at least three times.

Then he said, "Ben, I was not worried about this one mote. You have an A average and your letters of recommendations were great. Your SAT score was 1495 out of 1600. So, I am not surprised at all. I am so proud of you."

Ben said, "Thank you sir. I must admit that I'm a little scared."

Mr. Cason said, "That is expected. You are going to a new place without your family. Just like when you started working for me, do your best and everything will fall into place. Your best is far better than a lot of people. I look forward to hearing about everything when you come home to visit."

Ben smiled and said, "Yes sir!"

9

GRADUATION DAY

The next few months flew by; it was time for graduation. This is the big day everyone had been waiting for. Ben had attended the integrated school for three years. Initially, the school tried to keep down racial issues and treat everyone the same. However, there were still some separate but equal issues. There were two homecoming queens: one white, one black. There were two valedictorians: one white and one black. Now it was 1975 and the school board decided that there would be only one valedictorian, one salutatorian, homecoming queen, etc.

Of the 109 students, seven were considered honor graduates. They all had A averages for the four years of high school. So, the ranking was determined by the actual numeric grade that was given in each subject. Every point counted. Ben Davis was ranked third with an average of 96.5 over four years. The white valedictorian had an average of 97.1, the white salutatorian had an average of 96.7.

Ben walked into the golf shop for work afterschool, Mr. Cason had a big smile on his face.

Ben stated, "Mr. Cason, you're very happy today."

Mr. Cason said, "Yes, I am. I already heard that you are ranked third in your graduating class and will be saying the prayer at graduation."

Surprised Ben asked, "How did you hear? I wanted to tell you myself."

Mr. Cason said, "Ben, good news travels fast. The deputy was at the school today and they were talking about it in the office. He stopped by to tell me."

Ben laughed and asked, "Did he tell you that my prayer has to be three minutes long."

Mr. Cason said, "Yes, he did. He also said that you can read a scripture from the Bible before you pray."

Ben laughed and said, "Well, I guess you have heard the news!"

Mr. Cason said, "I could not be prouder of you. The whole town is. They are happy to see a black teenager be recognized for his accomplishments. Susie from the dry cleaners came down and asked me if it was true. She said that she heard it from Dave at the Western Auto."

Still surprised Ben said, "Wow, I never knew people talked about me."

Mr. Cason said, "Ben, you established a reputation when you started to work for me. So many people complimented me on the work that you did in the shop. Everybody knows who you are. Always remember our reputation precedes us. So, make sure you do things that will give you a good reputation, not a bad."

Ben laughed and said, "Yes sir. Graduation is on Saturday, May seventeenth at four o'clock in the afternoon on the football field. That is only a week or so away."

Mr. Cason said, "That is fine. I plan to close the shop that day. Tell your family that I will pick them up at 3:15."

Ben said, "Thanks Mr. Cason, I have to be at the gym at 2:30 pm, so now I won't have to worry about them."

Mr. Cason said excitedly, "No problem. I want us to get a good seat. I bought one of those Polaroid cameras, a Kodak camera, and a lot of film from the drug store. I want to take pictures."

Ben walked over to Mr. Cason and hugged him.

Then he said, "Thank you so much for everything."

Mr. Cason said, "You have brought me pure joy. Everything I have done for you is nothing in comparison to what you have given me."

Ben wiped the tears from his cheeks, then went to the storage room to start work. After work, Ben rushed home to tell his mother the good news. As he turned down Washington Street, there were his siblings waiting for him.

David announced, "I cooked pork chops for dinner today. I made some rice and we had some collards left over from the weekend."

Ben said, "That sounds delicious. I have great news, but I want to wait until Mom comes home to tell everyone."

Mary asked, "OK, does it have to do with your class ranking?"

Ben answered, "Yes, I don't want to say anything else."

David said, "OK, since it's good news. Let me go see what desert I can fix really fast as a celebration. You know I like celebrations!"

David rushed to the kitchen, Mary ran out the door to meet Mom. Ben went to the restroom to freshen up. Mom and Mary entered the door laughing.

Mom said, "David, you can smell those pork chops down the street. They smell delicious."

David laughed and said, "I'm glad. I tried something different this time."

Mary said, "Ben has good news, but he wanted to wait until you came home to tell us."

Mom said, "Good news. I love hearing good news. Let me go to the restroom to wash my hands and I will meet you all at the table."

Everyone was seated at the table when Mom entered the dining area. It was Ben's turn to say grace. Ben prayed for the family, their future, and the food.

Mom said, "Ben, that was beautiful prayer."

Then she started with her inquisitions, she asked, "Mary, how was your day?"

Mary said hastily, "It was great Mom. I pass. I want to hear Ben's good news."

Mom laughed out loud, then she asked, "David, how was your day?"

David eagerly said, "It was great Mom. I pass too. I want to hear Ben's good news."

Mom said, "OK, Ben tell us what your good news is."

Ben smiled and said, "Mom, as you know the student with the highest-grade point average (GPA) for the graduating class is the valedictorian, and the one with the next highest is the salutatorian. I'm ranked third in my graduating class. My GPA for the past four years is 96.5. In response to it being so high, they have asked me to say the prayer during the commencement."

Mom said, "That is good news! Now in the past, who has said the prayer?"

Ben said, "They would have a local minister pray."

Mom said, "Now that is an honor. So, you will make a speech just like the valedictorian and the salutatorian."

Ben said, "Yes ma'am, I get to speak for three minutes. They get to speak for four minutes."

Mom stood up and said, "That is great news. It's better than a regular speech because you get to give God glory. Wow! During grace you said a beautiful prayer, I know you will do a wonderful job on that day."

David asked, "Are you nervous?"

Ben said, "A little! Even though I took a speech class last year, I still have not had much practice speaking in front of a crowd."

Mary said, "My English teacher said, that when you speak in public, all you have to do is make sure you are prepared. She said when you are prepared, that it will overcome a lot of your nervousness."

Ben said, "I've never heard that. Well, I have one week to get prepared. Mr. Harris is our Senior Consultant, he said that I can write out my prayer and read it from the podium."

David said, "Just make sure you look up and don't keep your eyes on your paper. I hate it when someone is supposed to be speaking and they read to me."

Ben said, "Great point. Mom, what do you think?"

Mom said, "I think it's wonderful. I'm so proud of you. Not only because you have done well in school, but because of the young man you have become. I don't know what else to say. God's hand is on you Ben. This is just the beginning of great things in store for you."

Ben said, "Mr. Cason said for you all to be ready at 3:15 pm on Saturday. He will pick you up for the graduation ceremony on May seventeenth."

Mom said, "That's really nice of him. We will be ready."

Mary asked, "Mom, can I wear one of my church dresses?"

Mom said, "Yes you can, David, I want you to wear a shirt and tie."

David replied, "No problem. I bought a new tie last month. It's a bow tie"

Everyone laughed.

On graduation day Mom was up early fixing breakfast. She had already ironed Ben's white dress shirt and black pants twice. She also ironed his graduation gown and the honor cords.

Since the golf shop was closed, everyone sat down to have breakfast together. David talked about his weekly orders for cakes. Since that first Holiday Bake sale, he had orders for at least five cakes a month. If there was a holiday, he had many more.

David said, "I baked you a graduation cake. So, after the ceremony we can all come back here and celebrate."

Ben said, "Thanks! That's a great idea."

Mom said, "Ben, I know our family is small, but know that our church and our neighborhood is very proud of you."

Ben said, "Yes ma'am. Yesterday when I was walking home from work, Miss Bessie was waiting on the porch for me. She gave me two dollars and told me she was very proud of me."

Mom said, "That was very nice of her. People at the factory took up a collection for you too. They wanted me to give it to you after the ceremony."

Mary exclaimed, "Wow!"

Mom said, "Graduating from high school is a big thing and to graduate with honors is a really big thing. Then to get a full scholarship to a predominately white university is a bigger thing. That's why people are so proud of him."

David said, "I have been working hard in school too, I want to be just like Ben."

Mom said firmly, "David! Mary! All I want is for each of you to do your best. You don't have to be like anyone else. You are great when you do your best. Ben's best may not be your best. Your best may be better than Ben's best. All I ask is that you do the best you can do. Don't put pressure on yourself to measure up to someone else. Just be you! Be you at your best. Understand?"

David and Mary said, "Yes ma'am."

Ben left the house early to walk to the high school for graduation. He did not want to rush and get musty. All seniors were supposed to meet in the gym at 2:30 pm. He arrived at the gym before 2:00 pm. The gym was already half full of students. There were 109 graduating seniors. Excitement was in the air. Only ten percent of the class planned to go to college and twenty-five percent planned to go into the military. The other sixty-five percent planned to enter the workforce. Some had plans to move to Atlanta or some other big city to get a job.

Ben was not nervous, he was prepared. He had practiced his prayer every day, several times a day. He practiced his eye contact, moving his head from left to right, and using his finger to guide him on the paper. He was ready. He had written his scripture on paper, so he would not have to fumble through the Bible.

All of the graduates were lined up in alphabetical order. This was the day everyone had been waiting for. It was time for the ceremony to start. As they walked to the football field, Ben looked around. The sun was behind the clouds. There was a slight breeze in the air, it was about eighty degrees, cool for this time of the year. It was very comfortable outside even with the graduation gowns on.

As the graduates marched onto the football field everyone stood up. The bleachers were packed. He looked hard to locate his family, but he could not see them. The graduates took their seats on the football field. A stage had been built with special seats for the faculty and principal.

As Ben sat in his seat he thought about his life and how God had blessed him. Yes, his father died when he was ten years old. His mother had provided for his family and worked hard to instill values, manners, work ethic, and love in her children. Mr. Cason had been the father figure that he needed. He wiped the tears from his eyes. The prayer was the second item on the agenda, so he prepared himself.

As he walked up the steps that led to the stage, he looked out at the graduating class, then over to the bleachers where the community was seated. He still could not see his family, because there were so many people. Before he prayed, he said the following words.

"Good evening everyone. My name is Benjamin Davis. I stand before you today excited about my future, but saddened that I have to leave this community to pursue my dreams. As I look to my left I see a reminder of the high school days, but as I look to my right, I see the future that God has for each of us. A future of equality, community support, and family love. I would like to read Philippians 4:11-13"

11 Not that I speak in respect of want: for I have learned, in whatsoever state I am, therewith to be content.

12 I know both how to be abased, and I know how to abound: everywhere and in all things, I am instructed both to be full and to be hungry, both to abound and to suffer need.

13 I can do all things through Christ which strengthens me.

Ben continued, "We know not what the future holds, but we know that through Christ we will be strengthened to endure. Please bow your head with me in prayer:"

"Lord, we thank you for today, we thank you for bringing us to this point of commencement. We thank you for the school staff, our teachers, parents, and loved ones that have helped us to reach this point. Lord, we ask that you forgive us for any injustice that we have in our hearts, create in us a clean heart, so that we may receive the blessing you have in store for us".

"Lord, we cast all of our fears and cares on you; give us peace as we take the necessary steps to improve. Lord, we thank you for each and every person you have used to mold and shape us into the person you would have us to be."

"Lord, we know not what the future holds, but we trust you. We trust that you will guide us to each open door and close the doors that are not meant for us to enter. Lord, we ask for your protection, your strength, and your peace as we embark on our future outside of these school walls."

"Lord, we thank you for every opportunity and ask you to gird us up as we follow your path."

"We thank you for bringing us to this point of graduation and ask that you continue to guide us as we become productive citizens of this world. In Jesus name, I pray. Amen."

As he finished his prayer, everyone in the bleachers clapped and shouted. The members of his graduating class all clapped and smiled at him. As he walked off the stage, the principal, vice principal, and superintendent of schools all shook his hand. He smiled and returned each handshake with a firm grip. The applause was still going on as he sat in his seat. He could not believe it.

The classmate seated next to him leaned over and said, "Great job Ben!"

Ben said, "Thanks. I was nervous."

The classmate said, "You never would have known it."

The program continued with the valedictorian and salutatorian speeches. The students did well, however no one received the level of applause and support as Benjamin Davis.

After the ceremony, Ben rushed to the fence line that separated the football field from the bleachers. He was looking for his family. He was constantly interrupted by people who wanted to congratulate him and shake his hand.

Finally, he was able to make eye contact with Mr. Cason. Mr. Cason nodded his head. He used both of his hands to signal to Ben to 'slow down'.

Ben understood the gesture and slowed down and embraced the people who were congratulating him. His family waited patiently and marveled at the sight before them. When Ben finally reached them, they all hugged him at one time. Ben cried, his mom was crying, Mr. Cason was crying, David was trying not to cry, and Mary could not stop jumping up and down. They hugged each other what seemed to be a very long time.

Mr. Cason finally broke away and said, "Ben, this is a happy day. Not only are we proud of you, but the entire community of Fairville is too."

In awe Mom said, "I can't believe what just happened. I have never seen or heard anything like it. Of course, we know how awesome you are Ben, but you have established a reputation that everyone else knows too. I'm so proud of you."

Mr. Cason said, "You're right Phyllis. I have been to other graduations where students have done well in the school but they were braggarts and ignoble. No one could deny their achievements, but they were not embraced as Ben was today."

David said, "This is awesome. People congratulated me because I'm your brother."

Everyone laughed.

Mary exclaimed, "I can't stop smiling. I'm so happy for you Ben. What are we going to do next?"

Mom said, "David made a cake and some punch; so, let's go home and continue to celebrate."

Mr. Cason said, "That sounds like a plan. Before we go, let's get some pictures."

Mr. Cason took pictures then passed the camera to David for him to take some too. Everyone enjoyed the moment.

Then Mr. Cason asked, "Does anyone remember where we parked?"

Excitedly Mary exclaimed, "I do. Follow me!"

As everyone walked to the car, people continued to congratulate Ben not only on his heartwarming speech but his scholarship. Everyone wanted to shake his hand; some gave him money.

David had decorated the house with balloons and crepe paper. The living room looked very festive. Mr. Cason took more pictures. Neighbors stopped by to celebrate. When Mr. Cason left to go home it was almost 9:00 pm. It was a wonderful day.

10

PREPARING TO LEAVE FOR COLLEGE

The next day while at church, Reverend Otis King, the pastor, made an announcement telling everyone about Ben's accomplishments. Of course, everyone already knew. The congregation took up a collection to give to Ben. Reverend Otis invited Ben to say a few words.

Ben said, "I am overwhelmed. I appreciate all of your support not just today, but all of my life. I have grown up in this church and I am who I am today because of it. Of course, I will only be an hour and a half away. So, when I come home, you know I will be back in church on Sunday. Thank you again. Please continue to pray for me that I follow the path that God has set for me."

After church, more people shook Ben's hand. He slowed down and enjoyed the moment, but he had to go to work!

Then Mr. Knowlton said, "Ben, I know you have to go to work. I can give you a ride."

Ben said, "Thank you so much. I was going to be late."

Ben kissed his mother and said goodbye.

While in the car, Mr. Knowlton said, "Ben, you know

we are all very proud of you. When you get to college, it's not going to be easy. I want you to continue to do your best. Yes, Middle Georgia State University is integrated, but not everyone is going to embrace you. So, when you feel the stress of racial discrimination, just pray and trust God."

Ben said, "Yes sir. I'm a little nervous, but I'm ready."

Mr. Knowlton said, "I know you will be fine. I just want you to be prepared. Some discrimination may be slight, like not grading your homework fairly or changing the deadlines. So, stay aware of deadlines and make sure you do not wait until the last minute. You will have a dean for your area of study. If you feel any discrimination, don't hesitate to tell someone."

Ben asked, "Won't that make it worse?"

Mr. Knowlton said, "I hope not. God will show you who you can trust. Let God lead you."

As the car stopped in front of the golf shop, Ben said, "Thank you for everything Mr. Knowlton. If it were not for you, I could not have completed all of those forms."

Mr. Knowlton smiled and said, "That's what I'm here for. See you later."

Ben got out of the car and waved goodbye. As he entered the golf shop Mr. Cason was standing at the counter.

Mr. Cason said, "Ben, I expected you to be late today."

Ben said, "I almost was, but Mr. Knowlton gave me a ride. The people at the church took up a special collection for me, so I had to stay and shake everyone's hand."

Mr. Cason said, "That's great. I know they are proud of you too."

Ben said, "Yes sir. This is somewhat overwhelming. It's a good overwhelming."

Mr. Cason said, "I'm sure it is. Well, you are out of school, so you will be working forty hours a week now. Correct?"

Ben said, "Yes sir. I get to check into the dorm on Saturday, August sixteenth."

Mr. Cason asked, "Have you had a chance to visit the university?"

Ben said sadly, "No sir!"

Mr. Cason suggested, "Why don't you contact the university to see if we can come and visit some time during June. We all can drive up and take a tour of the campus."

Ben exclaimed, "That would be great Mr. Cason. Thanks!"

As Ben hugged Mr. Cason, he buried his head in his neck and shoulder area. Mr. Cason hugged him back with so much love that Ben almost cried.

Ben said, "I better get to work. We took yesterday off."

Throughout the day customers came in and congratulated Ben. Mr. Cason was so proud. Ben was able to arrange for a tour of the university campus on Saturday, June fourteenth. Everyone piled into Mr. Cason's car. Mr. Cason asked Ben to drive. The trip to Macon was enjoyable. Everyone talked in the car; it made the time go by fast.

Ben did not know where the campus was, Mr. Cason told him to ask for directions at the Gulf filling station. They were in the right vicinity; the campus was only five miles north. As they reached the campus, everyone awed at the large buildings and beautiful grounds.

Mom said, "I have never seen anything like this. It's almost palatial."

Mr. Cason said, "I have been to a few colleges; however, this landscaping is beautiful."

Ben parked the car at the visitor center. He went to check in. The people were very nice to him. He told them that his family was with him for the tour and that one of them is older and probably could not walk the entire campus.

The tour guide said, "We have a golf cart that we can use to take everyone around in."

Ben exclaimed, "That would be great."

Ben introduced himself and his family to the tour guide.

She greeted everyone and said, "My name is Tammy. I will be your tour guide for the day."

As they toured the campus, it was much bigger than Ben had anticipated.

Mr. Cason asked, "How many students attend this college?"

Tammy replied, "The campus does seem large. However, we only have a population of about 4,000 students."

Mary asked, "Do foreign students attend this university?"

Tammy said, "Yes, we do have some international students from all over the world. Some are from Africa, India, Europe, and Asia."

Mary said, "I'm not a xenophobic?"

Mr. Cason laughed and asked, "Mary, what does that word mean?"

Everyone laughed.

Mary said proudly, "Xenophobic means to be prejudice or dislike strangers from a foreign land. I just learned that word last week."

Everyone laughed.

Tammy pointed out the library, the student center, the cafeteria, and gym.

Mary asked, "How many floors does that library have?"

Tammy answered, "It only has three floors."

Mary said, "I can't imagine a building with three floors filled with books."

Everyone laughed.

Tammy then asked, "Ben, do you know what dorm you have been assigned to?"

Ben said, "Yes, I am assigned to Martin Hall."

Tammy said, "That is our next stop. Martin Hall is the male dorm. Most of the freshmen stay on the third floor. Have you been assigned a roommate?"

Ben answered, "I have not received any information about a roommate."

Tammy asked, "Would you like to see one of the dorm rooms?"

Ben answered, "Yes, please. I'm still trying to figure out what I need to bring."

Tammy stated, "You should receive a list in the mail detailing what items you need to bring. Since you are here, I can get you a copy."

After Tammy parked the golf cart, everyone got out and went into the lobby of the dorm.

Mom said, "This is a nice building. Is there a curfew for students?"

Tammy said, "Yes ma'am. The curfew is midnight for all students. Each dorm has a dorm coordinator. That person is available to assist the students with any of their housing needs. Each floor has a resident assistant. If you have any housing problems, you are to contact your resident assistant first."

As they walked into one of the dorm rooms, David said, "This is a small space."

Looking around Ben said, "Well, I guess all I need is a bed, a closet, and a dresser."

Mr. Cason asked, "Where are the restrooms?"

Tammy said, "There are two gang restrooms on each floor. There are ten showers in each rest room. There are also several toilets and sinks."

Mom walked around the room and said, "David, this room is bigger than the room you and Ben share."

Everyone laughed.

Mary said positively, "I think this room is very nice. You and your roommate will become good friends."

Mr. Cason said, "Mary, I agree."

Tammy said, "Yes, these rooms are a little small. However, I was very comfortable, after I took home all of the stuff I did not need."

Everyone laughed.

Ben said, "OK, I won't overpack!"

Tammy asked, "Ben, what is your major?"

Ben replied, "Business!"

Tammy said, "That's my major too. I will be a junior in the fall. I really enjoy business. I have found the professors to be very informative and patient."

Mr. Cason asked, "Have you heard of much discrimination here on campus?"

Tammy replied, "Unfortunately, there have been some cases. The university works hard to handle those cases and provide an equal opportunity environment for all students."

Mr. Cason said, "That is good. I don't want to have to come back up here for any issues, because I will."

Everyone laughed.

The last stop on the campus tour was one of the classroom buildings.

Tammy stated, "This is the College of Business building. All of your business classes will be in this building. However, during your first year when you are taking your common courses, you will be in classrooms all over the campus. So, make sure you have comfortable walking shoes."

Ben laughed and said, "I will. This is a beautiful building."

Everyone oohed and awed.

Tammy said, "This is one of our newest buildings. It was just completed in 1974. So, everything is new and improved."

Mom said, "The classrooms don't look that big. What is the average class size?"

Tammy said, "Our average class size is twenty-five students for most business classes. However, there are a few classes on campus where the class size can be fifty to seventy-five students. I have been here two years. So far, all of my classes have been small."

David asked, "Do you have a lot of females that attend this university?"

Tammy laughed and said, "Yes we do. It is currently fifty-five percent male and forty-five percent female."

Mr. Cason laughed and asked, "David, why are you worried about girls here?"

David laughed and said, "I wanted to know so when I come to visit!"

Everyone laughed.

When the tour was over, everyone stood around the visitor center just taking in the sights.

Mr. Cason said, "David, I think there is a camera in my trunk. Please get it, so we can take some pictures."

David retrieved the camera and Tammy took a photo of the family, standing in front of the building that said 'Welcome to Middle Georgia State University.' Everyone said goodbye and got in the car.

When Ben turned the corner to get back on the main road to exit the campus, Mary said, "Look, they have a bank just like ours in Fairville."

Mr. Cason said, "Yes, that's another branch of First National Bank of Georgia. You will find that there are branches all over the state."

Mary said, "I didn't know that. I thought our bank was one of a kind."

Ben said, "No, the bigger the bank is; the more branches it has in different areas or cities."

The drive home was full of chatter; everyone was excited about what they had seen. Mary talked about the big library full of books. David wondered what type of food they served in the cafeteria. Mom could not get over how beautiful the landscaping and buildings were. Mr. Cason denoted some of the differences between high school and college.

The next few months flew by. Mr. Cason and Ben talked about making friends, girls, college parties, illegal drugs, and everything else. Ben knew that Mr. Cason was very proud of him, but he also knew that Mr. Cason was going to miss him when he left.

One afternoon Ben asked, "Mr. Cason, do you need to hire anyone else, while I'm at college?"

Mr. Cason said, "Ben, that is a great question. Truthfully, I don't think I ever want to work with anyone else. No one could live up to your work ethic or tenacity. I think that I can handle it on my own. Now, that you have organized the storage room, created an inventory system, set up a monthly ordering system, and a monthly delivery schedule. I can maintain it."

Ben smiled and said, "Since college is only an hour and a half away. I was thinking that I would come home regularly to check on my family and I can check on you and the store to make sure everything is running OK."

Mr. Cason said, "That sounds wonderful. I would love that. I have also been thinking about transportation for you. How do you plan to get back and forth to Macon?"

Ben said, "I checked with the Greyhound Bus station in town. There is a bus that runs Wednesday, Friday, and Sunday.

It goes non-stop to Macon. Then I found out there is a city bus, that will take me from the bus station to the campus. It runs every day on the hour from seven o'clock in the morning until nine o'clock in the evening."

Impressed Mr. Cason said, "You have done some great research. That sounds good, but I think I have a better solution."

Ben stopped working and looked at Mr. Cason.

Mr. Cason continued, "Ben, you're a good driver."

Ben said, "Thank you sir, you taught me well."

Mr. Cason said, "You know I have those two trucks out back. I bought them in 1970, so they are not that old. You have cleaned them up so well; they look brand new."

Ben smiled.

Mr. Cason continued, "I have given this a lot of thought and I want to give you one of those trucks. Then you will have transportation for whatever you need and you won't have to catch the bus."

Ben exclaimed, "Mr. Cason, that's too much!"

Putting his hand up to silence Ben, Mr. Cason said firmly, "No, it is not! I don't know why I bought two in the first place. They have just been sitting out there in the back. Now, that you have set up a delivery system, I really only need one truck. So, you can have the other one. Let's consider it a graduation gift."

Ben wiped the tears from his face and said, "Mr. Cason, I can't accept it."

Mr. Cason said, "Nonsense! I look at it like the truck has been saved for you all along. Which one do you want: the brown truck or the blue one?"

Ben ran to Mr. Cason and hugged him tight, burying his head in his neck and shoulder area.

Ben asked, "Mr. Cason, why have you been so good to me?"

Mr. Cason smiled and said, "That's easy Ben, because you have been so good to me."

Wiping his tears Ben said, "I would love to have the blue one. That's my mom's favorite color."

Mr. Cason said, "Then the blue one is yours. I will continue to carry the insurance and fix any repairs that need to be done. I will also add your name to the registration so if you are stopped by the police, no one will think you stole the truck."

Ben laughed and said, "Mr. Cason, you think of everything."

Mr. Cason said, "There is one more thing I need you to do. I updated some paper work and Hank Jennings needs you to sign some more documents. So next week we can go over, OK?"

Still wiping the tears from his face, Ben said, "Yes sir. I better get back to work or I won't finish burnishing the display today."

Mr. Cason said, "I will be back, watch the store."

Mr. Cason left the store, he wanted to check with the local bank to see if it was true about blacks not being able to open an account.

As he entered the bank, the teller said, "Hello Mr. Cason. How are you today?"

Mr. Cason said firmly and seriously, "I am well. I have a question. What is your policy about opening an account here at the bank?"

The teller proudly said, "Sir, our policy recently changed on January 1, 1975. We now allow all races to have an account here at First National Bank of Georgia."

Mr. Cason asked, "Is there an age requirement?"

The teller said, "Yes sir, if they are under the age of eighteen, they must have an adult on the account with them?"

Mr. Cason asked, "Is that for checking and savings accounts?"

The teller answered, "Yes sir."

Mr. Cason asked, "Suppose I wanted to add someone to all of my accounts. What is the procedure?"

The teller said, "We would just need that person's signature on the signature card and we could add them to your accounts."

Mr. Cason asked, "Can those signature cards be signed at Hank Jennings office?"

The teller said, "Yes sir, they can. We do that all the time. Mr. Jennings would just have to request the signature cards. We will prepare them and they can be signed in his presence."

Mr. Cason said, "Thank you, you have been very helpful."

Mr. Cason walked back to the golf shop, Ben was checking out a customer and there were five customers waiting in line. Business had improved ten-fold since Ben was hired. Before then, Mr. Cason was lucky to get fifteen customers a week. Since Ben had been working at the shop, people from not only Fairville, but neighboring cities were coming to the shop. Ben took great care of the customers, walked each to the door, and waved goodbye.

When the store was finally empty, Mr. Cason asked, "Ben, do you still keep your savings in that coffee can?"

Ben smiled and said, "Yes sir. I have been working here for almost three years, I have saved nearly $600."

Mr. Cason said, "Ben that is great. I only pay you $1.60 an hour. Is that after you give your mother money to help out?"

Ben said, "Yes sir. That is also after I paid ten percent in tithes. With the money that people gave me for graduation, I have a little over $700."

Mr. Cason asked curiously, "Ben, what are tithes?"

Ben answered, "Tithes are the ten percent of your earnings that you give back to God. I pay my tithes at my church every time I get paid."

Mr. Cason said, "You have managed your money very well."

Ben said, "Thank you sir! It seems that no matter how much I spend, I seem to have more left over. Mom said that is a result of God's faithfulness."

Mr. Cason said, "I'm sure it is. I have noticed that since I hired you, I have done more business too. Have you noticed that some of the customers are from other cities?"

Ben said, "Yes sir, I have. I started making a mailing list of the customers. Maybe one day we can mail something to them."

Mr. Cason said, "That's another great idea! While I was out, I checked with the bank. As of the first of this year, they now allow people of all races to open a bank account. Would you like to open a savings account? You can't take a coffee can to college."

Ben laughed and said, "You're right. Do you remember that Mary saw a branch of our bank near the campus?"

Mr. Cason said, "I remember, so it would be very convenient for you."

Ben said, "I need to ask my mom, but I'm sure it would be OK with her."

Mr. Cason said, "Great! Ask her tonight. We can go over there tomorrow."

After work, Ben drove his blue 1970 Ford F-150 truck home. When he turned down the road to go home, David and Mary were waiting for him. He stopped the truck and they got in.

Mary asked, "Why are you driving Mr. Cason's truck?"

Ben said excitedly, "Can you believe that Mr. Cason gave it to me; this is my graduation gift!"

David exclaimed, "What! That's amazing. I can't believe it."

Mary said, "Mom is going to flip out. Do you think she will let you keep it?"

David said, "I think she will, Mr. Cason has been part of our family for almost three years."

Ben said, "I think she will let me keep it too. Mr. Cason said, that now I can come home when I want to or need to. I don't have to catch the bus."

Ben parked the truck in front of the house. David rushed to the kitchen to finish dinner. When it was time for Mom to come home, they all met her at the end of the road. When Mom turned the corner, they all hugged her. Mary took her work bag and they all laughed as they walked home. Mom saw the truck parked in front of the house.

She asked, "Isn't that Mr. Cason's delivery truck in front of the house?"

David grinned and said, "Yes ma'am, that is one of his trucks."

Mom questioned, "I wonder why he did not drive his car?"

Ben said excitedly, "Mom, Mr. Cason gave me that blue 1970 Ford F-150 truck as a graduation gift."

Acting surprised Mom asked, "What?"

Ben said, "Yes ma'am. He did. He said that now I can go to college and come home when I want to or need to without catching the bus."

David asked, "Mom, are you mad?"

Mom laughed and said, "How can you be mad at Mr. Cason. He loves Ben so much. He loves all of us. He has proven that so many times. Anyway, he asked me the other day if I had a problem with him giving Ben the truck. Of course, I didn't. I'm just overwhelmed with the blessings that God has sent our way."

Ben said, "Today, I could not stop crying. I'm overwhelmed

too. Mr. Cason said that he would continue to pay for the insurance and any repairs that are needed."

Mom said, "I'm speechless."

Ben said, "I asked Mr. Cason why has he been so good to me?"

Mom asked, "What did he say?"

Wiping back his tears Ben said, "Mom, he said, it's because I have been so good to him."

Mom reached over and hugged Ben. Mary and David all joined in with the hug.

Mom said, "Ben, God has blessed you through Mr. Cason. He has also blessed Mr. Cason through you. Wow! What a mighty God we serve."

Ben said, "Mr. Cason also said that the policy has changed at the bank. Now people of all races can open a bank account. He wanted your permission to open me a savings account at the bank."

Surprised Mom said, "Wow, that's great. How much money do you have saved in that coffee can?"

Ben proudly said, "With the graduation donations from everyone, I now have a little over $700."

Mom exclaimed, "Ben, I did not know that you had that much. You have done well in saving your money. Now, when you go off to college, you can buy some of the things you may need. That's wonderful!"

Ben laughed and said, "Mr. Cason said I should not take the coffee can to college."

David asked, "Can I have your coffee can to put my money in? I have about $110 profit from selling my cakes."

Everyone laughed and went in the house for another delicious dinner. After signing the paperwork at Mr. Jennings office and opening the savings account, the next few weeks flew by. It was finally Saturday, August 16, 1975. The day Ben was scheduled to leave for Middle Georgia State University.

Mom cooked a bountiful breakfast. Everyone laughed at the table. David was excited about the new culinary vocational classes that were available for juniors during the upcoming school year. Mary was excited about school starting and being able to take Latin in the eighth grade. After breakfast everyone helped Ben pack his suitcases and load the truck.

It was a very warm day; the sun was shining bright. The sky was blue with no chance of rain in the forecast. Mr. Cason drove up to say goodbye as everyone was standing in front of the house. Ben's truck was packed with things that were on the list and some things that were not on the list.

Mr. Cason thought about how his life had changed since he met Ben. Time was not on his side, so he prayed that God would allow him to live to see Ben graduate from college. Then Ben would be ready to receive all that he had planned, including his precious display case.

Interrupting his thought, he heard Mary say, "Ben, I hope you did not overpack, remember that dorm room is not that big."

Ben said, "I don't think I did. I plan to come home in about two weeks. So, if I have to bring something back, I can then."

Everyone laughed.

Mom said, "Ben, I thought I would be ready for this moment, but I'm not. I'm happy that you are going away to college; but I'm sad that I will not see you every day."

Mr. Cason said, "Phyllis, I know exactly how you feel. I feel the same way. My heart is breaking."

Wiping the tears from his face Ben said, "My heart is breaking too, but it's a good break. Part of me does not want to go. I want to stay here and continue to work at the golf shop.

The other part of me wants to go, so that I can learn all that I can and continue to make you both proud."

David said, "I did not think I would cry, but I'm going to miss you brother."

Mary said, "I always knew that I would cry. I was crying last night just thinking about you leaving."

Everyone hugged each other and cried.

Mr. Cason said, "You know how to take care of yourself and do your best. So, you will be fine. When you get there, please call me collect at the shop. We want to know that you arrived safely. Anytime you need anything, make sure you call."

Ben said, "Yes sir, I will."

Mom said, "I know it's only an hour and a half drive. I made you some sandwiches and put a few pieces of fruit in the bag. I was not sure if the cafeteria would be open today, when you get there."

Ben said, "Thanks Mom."

Ben hugged each of his siblings separately. He told each of them that he loved them and would see them soon. As he walked toward Mr. Cason, he could hardly console himself. He buried his head in Mr. Cason's neck and shoulder area. The more he cried, the more Mr. Cason cried. He pulled himself away and hugged his mother. By this time, he was crying even harder.

His mother hugged him tightly and prayed, "God, I ask you to protect my son while he is away. Lord, I ask that you encircle him in your hedge of protection, keeping him from any hurt, harm, or danger. Lord, I ask that you continue to open doors for him and close the doors that you do not want him to enter. God, I ask that you continue to order his steps in the path that you have set for him. God, I ask that you continue to provide all that he will need. In Jesus name I pray, Amen."

Everyone said, "Amen!"

Mom said, "Ben, wipe your tears and go with God. He is with you."

Ben held up his head and said, "Yes ma'am. I love you all."

Everyone said, "I love you too."

Ben got into the truck, buckled his seat belt, started the truck, and waved goodbye.

He said, "I will see you all in a couple of weeks."

Mr. Cason stood there proudly with his arm around Mom. David and Mary each waved goodbye as the truck went down the road. As he drove the truck down the road, Ben reflected on how his life had changed since he met Mr. Cason. The job had been saved for him; the truck had been saved for him. He wondered what else God had saved just for him.

To be continued…

Continue on this amazing journey with Ben as he discovers all that God has saved for him. Order today:

Book 1 Saved for Ben   ISBN 978-1-6642-6888-3
Book 2 Saved for Ben: The College Years ISBN 978-1-6642-6892-0
Book 3 Saved for Ben: Ben and Wanda   ISBN 978-1-6642-6895-1
Book 4 Saved for Ben: The Legacy   ISBN 978-1-6642-6898-2

Stay tuned for the continuing saga!

Printed in the United States
by Baker & Taylor Publisher Services